Return to Satterthwaite Court

"Wow. Just wow! Those who enjoy raillery and romance get ready to spar & swoon with Kate & Charles!"

—*Austenprose*

The Work of Art

"Matthews weaves suspense and mystery within an absorbing love story. Readers will be hard put to set this one down before the end."

—*Library Journal* (starred review)

"Strongly recommended."

—*Historical Novel Society*

Gentleman Jim

"Tartly elegant...A vigorous, sparkling, and entertaining love story with plenty of Austen-ite wit."

—*Kirkus* (starred review)

"Exhilarating...this page-turner shouldn't be missed."

—*Publishers Weekly* (starred review)

"Matthews ups the ante with a wildly suspenseful romance."

—*Library Journal* (starred review)

"*Gentleman Jim* is an utter delight."

–*Historical Novel Society*

The Lily of Ludgate Hill

"No one writes Victorian romance like Mimi Matthews, and her Belles of London series just keeps getting better!"

—Kate Quinn, *New York Times* bestselling author

"Mimi is truly a national treasure. All of her books are filled with such delicious chemistry and heart, and her writing is superb."

—Isabel Ibañez, #1 *New York* Times bestselling author

"It is truly a wonder how Matthews can consistently craft fresh romances featuring unique, multidimensional characters who face huge obstacles to their relationships."

— *Booklist* (starred review)

"Readers who love lots of intrigue and historicals that sound properly historical will savor this one."

—*NPR*

The Belle of Belgrave Square

"Shiveringly Gothic...Watching Julia blossom away from prying eyes is almost as satisfying as seeing Jasper Blunt pine for her from nearly the first page...For best effect, save this one for a windy night when trees scrape against the windowpanes."

—*New York Times Book Review*

"Mimi Matthews never disappoints."

—Jodi Picoult, #1 *New York* Times bestselling author

"Such tremendous good fun...Julian Fellowes fans will rejoice!"

—Kate Quinn, *New York Times* bestselling author

"This story unfolds like a rose blooming, growing more and more beautiful as each delicate layer is revealed. A tender, luminous romance."

—Caroline Linden, *USA Today* bestselling author

"A grand cross-class romance, a twisty mystery, and

emotional internal struggles combine to excellent effect in Matthews's effervescent second Belles of London romance."

"Mimi Matthews just doesn't miss."

"An intoxicating, suspenseful romance. Highly recommended."

The Siren of Sussex

"A tender and swoonworthy interracial, cross-class romance in Victorian London...Readers will delight in this paean to women's fashion and horseback riding."

"Romance aficionados who love fashion and animals will delight in this tender romance."

"Matthews brings the Victorian era to vivid life with meticulously researched details and an impossible romance made believable and memorable."

Fair as a Star

"Historical romance fans won't want to miss this."

—*Publishers Weekly* (starred review)

"A kindhearted love story that will delight anyone who longs to be loved without limits."

—*Library Journal* (starred review)

The Matrimonial Advertisement

"For this impressive Victorian romance, Matthews crafts a tale that sparkles with chemistry and impresses with strong character development...an excellent series launch."

—*Publishers Weekly*

"Matthews has a knack for creating slow-building chemistry and an intriguing plot with a social history twist."

—*Library Journal*

A Holiday By Gaslight

"Matthews pays homage to Elizabeth Gaskell's *North and South* with her admirable portrayal of the Victorian era's historic advancements...Readers will easily fall for Sophie and Ned in their gaslit surroundings."

—*Library Journal* (starred review)

"A graceful love story...and an authentic presentation of the 1860s that reads with the simplicity and visual gusto of a period movie."

The Lost Letter

"Lost love letters, lies, and betrayals separate a soldier from the woman he loves in this gripping, emotional Victorian romance."

"A fast and emotionally satisfying read, with two characters finding the happily-ever-after they had understandably given up on. A promising debut."

Books by Mimi Matthews

FICTION

Somerset Stories

The Work of Art

Gentleman Jim

Return to Satterthwaite Court

Appointment in Bath

A Lady of Conscience

Belles of London

The Siren of Sussex

The Belle of Belgrave Square

The Lily of Ludgate Hill

The Muse of Maiden Lane

Parish Orphans of Devon

The Matrimonial Advertisement

A Modest Independence

A Convenient Fiction

The Winter Companion

Victorian Romances

The Lost Letter

The Viscount and the Vicar's Daughter

Victorian Christmas Novellas

A Holiday By Gaslight

Victorian Romantics

Fair as a Star

Gothic Fiction

John Eyre

NON-FICTION

The Pug Who Bit Napoleon:

Animal Tales of the 18th and 19th Centuries

A Victorian Lady's Guide to Fashion and Beauty

A Lady of Conscience

SOMERSET STORIES
BOOK FIVE

MIMI MATTHEWS

A LADY OF CONSCIENCE
Somerset Stories, Book 5
Copyright © 2024 by Mimi Matthews

Cover Design by James T. Egan of Bookfly Design
Cover Photo by Lee Avison /Arcangel

E-Book: 978-1-7360802-7-6
Paperback: 978-1-7360802-8-3

For Bijou, who always follows her heart—
wherever it may lead her.

Prologue

Beasley Park
Somersetshire, England
January 1844

Hannah Heywood slipped out the kitchen door of Beasley Park, her hooded velvet cloak drawn up over her head against the winter chill. There was a full moon tonight. It shone, luminous as a pearl, in the midnight sky above, shimmering over the snow that covered the empty stable yard. She raised the small oil lantern she carried in her gloved hand, lighting the way to the stone stable block beyond.

After an evening of dancing and merriment, she'd been too restless to sleep. It didn't help that she hadn't successfully settled into her room. Her first night as a guest

1

at the grand West Country home of the Earl and Countess of Allendale had been marked by much tossing and turning, and this night promised to be no better.

She was missing her pets, of course. Hannah supposed it was to be expected. This was the first time she'd left them—*or* her parents—for any length of time. Worries had begun to plague her from almost the first moment she and her older brother, Charles, had departed Heywood House. Thoughts about Evangeline, her three-legged spaniel, refusing to eat, or about Tippo, her aged pug, whining at the door of her empty bedchamber for hours on end, waiting in vain for his young mistress's return.

They weren't overly sentimental imaginings. They were rational fears motivated by fact. Hannah knew her pets. She knew they would be pining.

But it was only for a day longer. She and Charles were traveling back to Heywood House in the morning, their brief stint as the guests of the vivacious Lady Kate Beresford, daughter of Lord and Lady Allendale, at an end.

Hannah was eager to return home. In the meanwhile, her restlessness was best assuaged by checking on the only animals of hers that were still readily within her control.

She let herself into the darkened stables. Her family's team of carriage horses—Dandy and Walter—had been housed inside since Hannah's arrival three days ago. Along with Evangeline and Tippo, they'd never been far from Hannah's thoughts during her stay. She made a point of personally looking in on them every day.

Each time she'd visited, it was always the same. They'd been comfortable, well-fed, and contented. It was no different on this occasion. Entering the stable, she found them dozing peacefully in their looseboxes, settled in for the night on thick beds of fresh straw. She was moving toward them, their names on her lips ("Walter! Dandy!"), when a sound arrested her step.

There was someone else in the darkness of the stable. A gentleman stood in front of one of the looseboxes at the end of the aisle, his tall, broad-shouldered frame just visible in the glow cast from her lamp.

Hannah's heart leapt into her throat. She recognized that icy blond profile. That height, those shoulders, and the adamantine firmness of that uncompromising chiseled jaw.

It was James Beresford, Viscount St. Clare.

Lord St. Clare was the eldest of Lady Kate's three older brothers. He was also, quite possibly, the handsomest gentleman Hannah had ever beheld. So disturbingly handsome that, from the minute they'd been introduced to each other, Hannah had found it difficult to look him in the eye.

It was childish, really. He'd been nothing but civil to her. Coldly, excruciatingly, civil.

But she'd felt his penetrating gray gaze on her at the dance this evening—both during the giddy, stomach-fluttering moments when they'd waltzed together, and during those moments when she'd been dancing with someone else.

No doubt he found her an oddity. Her mismatched blue and brown eyes were often an arresting sight to strangers, and her extreme shyness frequently put them off. Even the warmest people sometimes found it trying to converse with her. And Lord St. Clare was the very opposite of warm. He didn't laugh or jest like the rest of the

Beresfords. Indeed, he rarely spoke at all except when absolutely necessary, and then only with the strictest formality.

But there was nothing formal about him now.

He was in his shirtsleeves; absent the impeccably tailored evening coat and elegant black silk cravat he'd worn when he'd waltzed with her earlier that night. His golden-blond hair was mussed, his mouth curved in something like a scowl. He was out of countenance, possibly even angry—the tight hold he kept over his emotions temporarily relaxed because he'd believed himself to be alone.

She lowered her lamp, instinctively shrinking back into the shadows. There was little worse than intruding on a person's private moment, especially if that person was a frost-hearted viscount who prided himself on his unrelenting sense of control. He wouldn't thank her for having spied him without it. Quite the reverse.

But there was no hiding. Not now he'd seen her.

"Miss Heywood," he said coolly. He bowed to her in the darkness.

Hannah swallowed hard. Stiffening her spine, she made herself step forward, revealing her face to his view. "Lord St. Clare." She dropped a reflexive curtsy. "Good evening."

Unsettling as his presence was, it behooved her to stay on good terms with him. She doubted this would be her last visit to Beasley Park. Unless she was very much mistaken, her brother Charles was halfway to being in love with Lady Kate. Which meant that, eventually, the two of them would marry. It also meant that very soon Lady Kate's three brothers would be as good as family to Hannah.

One brother in particular.

Lord St. Clare came down the aisle to join her. "Dare I ask what you're doing out here at this time of night?"

I might ask you the same, Hannah nearly replied. But she wasn't one to banter. Neither was she an accomplished flirt. Her shyness prevented all but the barest conversation with strangers. Unless, that is, she was talking about her animals.

"I'm looking in on my horses before retiring," she said.

His gaze was inscrutable. "Had you reason for concern?"

"Only that they're in a strange place, far from home."

"You need have had no apprehension on that score. Our head groom is excellent."

"I'm certain he is, sir."

"Yet still you're here." He dropped an enigmatic glance down the front of her velvet cloak, to where the cloth gaped to reveal the silk gown beneath. "And still in your evening dress."

A flare of self-consciousness heated her cheeks. She drew her cloak more firmly about herself. "I-I was too restless to retire to my room after the dance," she said, stammering a little. "I've had no opportunity to change."

He looked at her steadily, his fathomless gray gaze impossible to read. "Ah yes. The dance. I'd almost forgotten."

Hannah's blush deepened. Naturally it hadn't meant anything to him. He was a gentleman of breeding and bearing. A man of five and twenty, far older in both age and experience than her meager nineteen years. The waltz they'd shared this evening had been a thrillingly romantic event to her, but one he'd plainly forgotten the instant the music had ended.

"I'm not accustomed to parties," she said in an effort to explain. "We live a quiet life at Heywood House. Even a small dance in a private drawing room is a great cause for excitement."

He joined her at the side of the loose box. His arm brushed lightly against hers as he cast a brief look in at Dandy. "Whatever the cause for your excitement, you may be assured your horses are content."

Her pulse fizzed at his touch, the same way it had fizzed when he'd taken her hand to dance with her. He wasn't a comfortable gentleman to be around by any means. His very proximity did odd things to her circulation.

She followed his gaze into the loose box, ignoring the quivering in her stomach. Dandy was snuffling in his sleep, one back foot cocked at rest. Hannah's mouth tilted up in a fond smile. "Yes, I see that now."

"You weren't genuinely worried, I trust."

"I always worry about my animals." She paused, struggling to explain in words what she so easily articulated in the letters and anonymous opinion pieces she wrote in support of the burgeoning animal welfare movement. "They can't speak for themselves, you see. Not in a way that human beings can readily understand. It's up to me to give them a voice. To be their advocate, if necessary."

Her words were met with a prolonged silence.

Hannah's growing sense of discomfiture increased exponentially. She supposed that, given her shyness, she didn't strike him as much of an advocate. Naturally he underestimated her. He knew nothing about the strength of her convictions or about the lengths she was willing to go to for a noble cause.

"An admirable philosophy," he replied at length.

She couldn't tell if that was sarcasm in his tone. "It's not a philosophy. It's a moral duty."

"Is that why you don't eat animal flesh?"

He was the first one of the Beresfords to ask Hannah about it outright. The others had merely accepted her dietary restrictions as a matter of course. Hannah suspected that her brother had privately addressed the matter with Lady Kate when they'd arrived, thereby avoiding any awkwardness with the menu during their stay—or any awkward questions.

But Hannah didn't mind questions about her principles. Not if they were asked in a spirit of sincerity.

"In large part, yes," she said. She'd given up eating meat several years ago, in consultation with her long-distance correspondent, Miss Mitra, and other female members of the movement. "It isn't exceptionable. Many in the world refrain from eating animals. The Hindu, for example."

Lord St. Clare's icy expression didn't change. Hannah nevertheless thought she detected a faint hint of incredulity at the back of his eyes. As though he'd expected her to be ignorant of the world or wholly immature—or both.

"I read books," she informed him. "And I correspond with all manner of interesting and well-informed people."

"Do you indeed?"

"I do. I'm a capital correspondent."

The barest trace of a smile shadowed the firm line of his mouth. "I'm sure that you are."

She drew back from him with a frown. She didn't like to be teased. Not by him. Not about something so serious as her feelings toward animals. "You think me amusing, I daresay."

Lord St. Clare met her eyes in the lamplight. "What I

think, Miss Heywood, is that your commitment to your beliefs shows a rather impressive largeness of mind."

She blinked. "Oh."

"I also think that if you remain out here for a moment longer in service to those beliefs, you're likely to catch your death."

"I'm perfectly warm in my cloak," she assured him. She hesitated before adding, "It's you I worry about."

His brows lifted slightly. "Me?"

"Do you often venture out into the snow without your coat or your neckcloth?"

"No. Not often." His forehead creased. He lapsed into silence again for several seconds before admitting, "I've just come from the library, and a heated exchange with one of my brothers. The snow was the best remedy for my temper. That and a visit with my stallion. A few moments in his company never fails to restore my equanimity."

Hannah nodded in immediate sympathy. She knew there had been tension in the house this evening, much of it owing to Lord St. Clare's younger brother, Ivo Beresford, having invited the daughter of an estranged neighbor to their family party.

"Horses have that talent," she said. "Troubles never seem so great when you're standing beside one of them. It's owing to their size, I believe. It dwarfs us, and our problems."

"Very well put."

"I contributed a brief article about the effect to a new journal on animal welfare that one of my correspondents is publishing in Bath. I mean to procure a copy for myself when next I visit."

He gave her another of his unfathomable looks. "You'll be traveling there in the spring?"

Hannah was surprised that he knew of her plans. She hadn't talked about her upcoming season in Bath during her visit, except when in company with Charles and Lady Kate. "It's to be my formal debut." She felt compelled to add, "London wouldn't have suited me. I prefer things to be simple."

"Don't we all." He offered her his arm. "If you will permit me to escort you back inside?"

She cast a last glance at Dandy and Walter before taking it. "Very well."

The muscles in Lord St. Clare's arm were powerful under the curve of her gloved hand, unhindered by the thick layer of his coat. He was an athletic gentleman. A man as strong in his body as he was in his self-restraint.

His composure had been wobbling tonight in the aftermath of his argument with his brother. A disconcerting sight. She wondered what it would look like if the viscount ever lost control completely. If he ever succumbed to the wild, reckless, passionate nature for which the Beresford family was rumored to be famous.

It wasn't likely to happen. And even if it did, Hannah wouldn't be around to see it. In the spring she would go to Bath, where she would meet and marry a sensitive, bookish gentleman, as unlike the cold-blooded viscount as night was to day. It was for the best. She required warmth in her life. She required joy. Despite the cracks she'd observed in his armor, Lord St. Clare didn't seem capable of either.

Back at the house, he held the kitchen door for her and waited as she preceded him inside.

She drew back the hood of her cloak, revealing the

plaited coiffure of her dark auburn hair. "Thank you, my lord," she said breathlessly. "I shall bid you goodnight."

"Sleep well, Miss Heywood."

"And you, sir." With that, she hurried from the kitchens, her heart beating heavily at her throat. She was certain she felt the weight of his lordship's gaze at her back, following her until she'd disappeared from his sight.

Chapter One

Bath, England
April 1844

"All roads lead to Bath," Charles Heywood observed.

Hannah scarcely registered her older brother's words. She was occupied staring out the window of their carriage as it traveled down Bennet Street toward the crowded Circus. Gently curving terraces of honey-colored limestone rose up alongside them. There were no harsh angles in Bath, only softness in both shade and form.

This wasn't her first experience of the city's beauty. Heywood House was but fifty miles from the fashionable watering place. She'd often visited as a child in company with her parents.

But Hannah wasn't a little girl on holiday this time. She was a young lady embarking on her very first season. Her stomach trembled as she took in the fashionably clad ladies and gentlemen strolling along the busy thoroughfare.

Anxiety had been plaguing her for weeks. Months, in truth. So much of her future hinged on her debut. The pressure of it was nearly too much to bear.

It shouldn't be this way. Not for a young lady of good family, with loving parents and a devoted brother to support her. It wasn't as though Hannah was being forced to find a husband. She needn't marry at all if she so chose. Both her mother and father had made that fact abundantly plain.

No. It was Hannah herself who had insisted on making her debut. Despite her shyness, despite the butterflies in her stomach and the apprehension buzzing in her veins, she was eager for her chance at romance. How could she not be? She had been an observer of romance all her life. Her parents were still deeply in love after decades of marriage. Her brother was in love too. His engagement to Lady Kate Beresford had been announced only last month.

"Have you heard a word I'm saying?" Charles asked from his place across from her.

Hannah let the tasseled velvet window curtain fall. Sinking back in her seat, she gave her brother her full attention. "Something about all roads leading to Bath?"

"I was talking about Kate," he said.

Hannah wasn't surprised. Her brother's thoughts had been on little else recently. "Mama said you received a letter from her yesterday afternoon."

"I did," Charles replied, frowning.

Hannah was immediately alert. "She's not in ill health?"

"No. Nothing like that. However... She did mention

that her family party will be larger than we originally expected."

Lady Kate was presently in Bath with her parents, the Earl and Countess of Allendale. Her middle older brother, Ivo, was there as well. Like his sister, he'd recently become engaged. That was the extent of the Beresford family party, as far as Hannah was aware.

Folding her gloved hands in her lap, she waited for Charles to explain.

"Her older brother has joined them unexpectedly," he said.

Hannah nodded. "Ivo, yes. I already know that."

"Not Ivo."

"Jack?" Hannah had met the youngest of Kate's older brothers on several occasions. At one-and-twenty, he was but two years older than Hannah was herself. He was also wild and unpredictable, more like a mischievous boy than a man fully grown.

"Not Jack," Charles said. "Her oldest brother, Viscount St. Clare."

Hannah's mouth went dry. She affected an air of unconcern. "Oh?"

As ever, Charles saw right through her. "I debated telling you. You've been anxious enough without having to worry about encountering him."

"Why should I worry?"

"He unnerves you."

Hannah inwardly grimaced. Was it that obvious? "I'm not likely to see much of him, am I?"

"That depends. I can't imagine him taking part in the season. Not in Bath. Kate expects him to remove to London in the coming weeks."

Hannah expected he would. Lord St. Clare's younger siblings had often made joking references about his exacting standards. According to them, his lordship's future wife must be a pattern card of perfection. Wealthy, pedigreed, beautiful, and accomplished. A young lady equipped to be a leader in fashionable society, and to one day take up the mantle of Countess of Allendale.

Which begged the question: if Lord St. Clare was seeking such an exemplar, why on earth had he come to Bath? The season here could in no ways compare with the one in London. Bath was shabbier in that respect. The parties smaller, the populace verging on elderly, and the quality of young ladies on offer more representative of lesser gemstones than diamonds of the first water.

Hannah counted herself among those gemstones. She felt no regret at the fact. She didn't aspire to be a diamond. Her temperament was ill-suited for that degree of attention. It was the entire reason she'd resolved to have her season here rather than in town.

"He'll doubtless call on us to pay his respects," Charles said. "Aside from that, you won't be bothered by him."

Hannah smoothed her gloves with restless fingers. "It's all one to me. I shall likely be too busy to take any notice."

Her brother smiled. "Mama mentioned shopping."

"Oh yes. We have ever so much to buy when she arrives." Hannah's parents would be joining them tomorrow, along with Hannah's dogs, Evangeline and Tippo, and her mare, Jubilee. "Until then, I have my own interests to pursue."

She had arranged to meet her friend, Miss Matilda Winthrop at Molland's Pastry Shop in Milsom Street in the morning. They had never yet met in person. Thus far, they had only ever corresponded by post. Miss Winthrop was a fierce advocate for animals. It was she who had undertaken to publish the new journal on animal welfare that Hannah had mentioned to Lord St. Clare.

"Animal interests, I presume," Charles said.

"Naturally."

"Just so long as you take care not to get into too much trouble."

"When have I ever got into trouble?" Hannah wondered.

"Never on your own behalf. But on an animal's account? Frequently."

"You would have done the same in the circumstances. And *have* done the same," she added, "many, many times."

"I'm not a young lady embarking on her first season."

Hannah gave her brother a reproving look. "Surely one can take part in the season without ignoring the dictates of one's conscience?"

"I'm not asking you to ignore your conscience," Charles said, "only to think twice before imperiling your reputation. Bath may be more forgiving than London, but you'll still be under scrutiny. Fashionable cities thrive on scurrilous gossip. It passes for entertainment. I'd rather you not find yourself the subject of it."

Her brother's words did nothing to ease Hannah's anxiety. She didn't like to imagine people gossiping about her. "I won't do anything to imperil my reputation," she assured him.

Not on purpose.

———— ❦ ————

James Aldrick Nicholas Beresford, Viscount St. Clare, handed his sister, Kate, down from the black lacquered carriage. He didn't agree with calling in Camden Place so early. Lieutenant Charles Heywood and his sister had only arrived in Bath half an hour ago. They'd scarcely had time to refresh themselves, let alone settle in.

It was Kate who had insisted on paying the untimely visit. She'd had a servant looking out for her betrothed's carriage since the early afternoon. The instant Kate had learned of his arrival, she'd insisted on setting off.

"We needn't stand on ceremony," she said to James. "We're practically family, after all."

James shot his sister a cooly repressive glance. Kate was the youngest child of the family, as well as being the only girl. She'd been shamefully spoiled as a consequence. Brash, bold, and unapologetically headstrong, it wouldn't occur to her not to give in to her wildest impulses.

It was a typically Beresford trait, this urge to charge ahead, come what may. Their family was known for being overpassionate. For fighting duels, engaging in fisticuffs, and generally throwing caution to the wind. It was something in their blood—a combustible combination of Beresford daring and (on his mother's side) Honeywell recklessness.

James had spent most of his life battling against it. It hadn't been easy. Indeed, it took a certain strength of will to rein in his passions. To think pragmatically, logically, rather than letting his heart run away with his head. The alternative hadn't been an option. There was already enough scandal attached to the family. He had no intention of creating more of it. Quite the opposite. As the heir to the earldom, James planned to rehabilitate the Beresford name.

"Not quite family, yet," he pointed out to his sister.

Kate shook out her striped silk skirts. Striding ahead of him, she rapped twice on the white-painted door. "Nonsense," she said. "Charles and I will be married before the summer is out. We've no cause for this tedious decorum."

James's face remained impassive as a liveried footman admitted them into the marble-tiled hall. Servants scurried past, hauling trunks up the stairs and carrying boxes down to the kitchens, under the direction of a stout, white-aproned housekeeper.

Among all the chaos, Charles Heywood strode forward to meet them. He was a tall, dark-haired fellow with a military bearing. Seeing Kate, his stern face was transformed by a smile. "This is excellent timing." He bowed to them before taking Kate's hands. "You must have had the watch out for us."

"I confess I did." Kate glanced behind Charles as he kissed her cheek in greeting. "Where is your sister?"

"Hannah is in her room, changing. She'll be down in a moment."

James cast an opaque look toward the curving staircase. He had last seen Hannah Heywood over a month ago when he and his family had traveled to Heywood House to celebrate Charles and Kate's engagement. Then, James had been in her company only briefly.

All *too* briefly.

The fact that Miss Heywood had been at her childhood home, comfortably surrounded by her family and her pets, had done little to alleviate her shyness where James was concerned. She'd rarely looked him in the eye, seeming more content to avoid him than to converse with him.

Such maidenish reticence in another girl would have been off-putting. In Miss Heywood, it had only served to intrigue him. Perhaps it was because her shyness wasn't the whole of her. Underneath her blushes, she was a young lady of peculiar conviction. She loved animals, and was prepared to fight for them, even if she couldn't yet summon the courage to speak up for herself.

James admired the impulse in her. The fact was, he was coming to admire her full stop. It was a devilish realization. They'd exchanged only a handful of words since first meeting at Christmas. Most of his opinions about her had been gleaned from observation. She was graceful. Thoughtful.

Beautiful.

And entirely ill-suited for the role of his future countess.

"Come and sit down in the drawing room," Charles said. He turned to the housekeeper. "Two more for tea, Mrs. Pritchett."

"Yes, Mr. Heywood," the housekeeper replied. She immediately returned to directing one of the footmen. "Not there! Those books belong in the library."

James trailed after Charles and Kate as they made their way upstairs to the expansive silk-papered drawing room. It was furnished in an opulent style, not vastly different from the drawing room in the Beresfords' own rented house near the Circus.

He seated himself in an armchair, somewhat removed from the damask sofa where Charles and Kate sat down together. James may not approve of his sister's impetuousness, but he wasn't a killjoy. He knew Kate had been missing her fiancé. The least James could do was keep his distance while the two of them enjoyed their reunion.

As they did, James boredly examined the grain of his expensive leather gloves. It was never quite comfortable to be around an engaged couple, especially when one was still unattached oneself. It required a certain appreciation for romance, which James was fully aware he was lacking.

He was supposed to have been the first among his siblings to become engaged. Instead, Kate had beaten them all to the wire, followed shortly by Ivo. As yet, Jack showed no signs of being headed in a similar direction. Still, it didn't sit well with James to have fallen so far behind in his duty to the title. By rights, he should be in London, searching out a suitable bride of his own. Not in Bath. And not here, in Camden Place, indulging his unfortunate attraction to a shy, West Country bluestocking.

Kate and Charles were still murmuring to each other, smiling and holding hands, when Miss Heywood entered the room. She was simply dressed in a gown of dove gray wool. Its snug bodice and close-fitting long sleeves accentuated the soft curves of her figure.

James was at once on his feet.

A soft, petal pink stain suffused Miss Heywood's cheeks as he bowed to her. She offered a polite curtsy in return.

"Hannah!" Kate rose to clasp Miss Heywood's hands. "How well you look!" She kissed her cheek. "I'm not at all surprised, though I know underneath you must be exhausted from your journey. Even fifty miles is a trial if one isn't used to traveling. You will be wanting to rest, I don't wonder. Come, sit down. I promise my brother and I won't stay overlong."

James said nothing. There was no room for him to speak, nor any cause for him to do so, not with Kate chattering so gaily. She resumed her seat on the sofa with Charles, urging Miss Heywood to the vacant chair next to James.

Miss Heywood took it, her eyes downcast and her face still coloring prettily.

James sat down beside her, separated from her by nothing more than the width of a low, polished wood table. Her profile was in his periphery; the dark arch of her winged brow, the elegant slope of her cheek, and the sweep of her thick, dark auburn hair, smoothed back into a simple knot at her nape.

"I've ordered tea for us," Charles said to his sister.

"Thank you," Miss Heywood replied.

It may well have been the first words she'd uttered since entering the room. The low, velvet murmur of her voice struck a disconcerting chord in James's chest.

He steeled himself against the feeling.

He had no tolerance for unfettered emotion. It provoked one to take inadvisable risks and to make foolish decisions. He'd seen the proof of it often enough in his family. For generations, the Beresfords' course had been navigated by a passionate star—to frequently perilous result. When it came to his own path, James was resolved to steer with his head rather than his heart.

Kate continued to cheerfully drive the conversation, talking about her impending wedding to Charles, and about Miss Heywood's upcoming season. It wasn't until the tea had been served and a portion of seed cake dutifully eaten that James's sister at last returned to her private, murmured discussion with her betrothed, leaving James and Miss Heywood to talk amongst themselves.

James looked at her steadily. She was focused on sipping her tea, her posture straight, her head bent gracefully, and her skirts spilling about her in a swell of soft gray wool. He suspected she was avoiding looking at him.

It was difficult for him to fathom such a profound degree of shyness. He'd met many young ladies in his five and twenty years. Even the most reserved among them had still been capable of polite conversation. At the very minimum, they had managed to meet his eyes.

He set down his tea cup. "Your journey was pleasant?"

"Yes, thank you," she said.

"And your parents? They follow behind you, I understand."

"They do." Miss Heywood slowly returned her own cup to its saucer. Her gaze lifted to his with an obvious effort, revealing her different colored eyes. They were beautifully expressive, soft and doe-like, and fringed with unusually long, black lashes. "My father had several estate matters to settle with his steward. We so rarely go away from home for any length of time. There was much to arrange."

James could well imagine. He presently had the charge of his parents' two largest estates. They employed stewards, of course, but it was James who worked in concert with them, not his father. When James wasn't in London, he spent his time travelling between Beasley Park, his mother's ancestral home in Somerset, and Worth House, the family seat in Hertfordshire, dealing with everything from crop and livestock management to structural improvements, recordkeeping, and contractual issues with farmers.

His late great-grandfather had hammered home the necessity of the future earl knowing his lands backward and forward. It wasn't enough to derive an income from one's property. A responsible landowner had a duty of care to his lands, and to every creature that subsisted upon them. James's father had learned it before him. And now it was James's turn. He'd taken up the reins not long after coming of age.

"My sister informs me that your mother is bringing your dogs to Bath," he said.

Miss Heywood's mouth lifted in a fleeting smile. "She is."

"They'll stay here with you for the whole of your season?"

"If all goes to plan. My brother took care to find a house that would be amenable to them." She cast a glance about the room, the single look seeming to encompass the entirety of the well-appointed property. "I hope they shall be content here. The garden is very small, and there is so little in the way of fields or pastures for them to frolic in."

"A lack of which will be amply offset by their happiness at being in your company," James replied gallantly.

Her blush deepened. "That's very kind of you to say."

"It's the truth, merely. When we visited your family last month, I saw for myself how fond your pets are of you."

"They are very dear to me," she said. "I was distressed at Christmas being away from them so long."

James remembered. Indeed, he had reflected on her brief visit to Beasley Park with alarming frequency in the intervening months. He and Miss Heywood had waltzed together, then. They had talked together too, with surprising candor. And not in a drawing room. It had been late at night, in the Beasley Park stables.

Miss Heywood had come to look in on her horses and found James there, in his shirtsleeves, still seething after a bitter argument with Ivo. On encountering him, she had plainly wanted to flee. Instead, she'd remained and talked with him, quietly, sensibly.

James had already been interested in her, albeit against his will. By the time they'd parted, he'd been something else. He didn't know how to define it. Whatever it was, it had been powerful enough to bring him to Bath.

"I trust you won't be distressed on this occasion," he said. "Not with your family and dogs in residence."

"Not in that respect, no."

He studied her face. "In other respects?"

Her eyes betrayed a glimmer of anxiety. "It's natural to be apprehensive about one's first season, is it not?"

"I couldn't say. I've nothing to judge it by but my sister's experience." James didn't expand on the remark. Little could be served by dredging up Kate's many scandals.

Miss Heywood glanced at his sister. "Kate has promised to help me while she's here."

"Indeed?"

"I know it cannot be for long. She departs for London with your parents at the close of next week. They have the wedding plans to attend to."

"I'm sure she would remain longer if she could."

"It is enough that she'll stay through my first ball. I'm resolved it will be a great success."

Another gentleman might have suavely replied that it was certain to be one, but James couldn't bring himself to lie, not even for politeness's sake. Miss Heywood's shyness was a liability. A potentially crippling one at that. If she intended to move in society with any degree of success, she would have to overcome it.

"You are to make your debut at Lord and Lady Carletons'?" he asked.

The elderly Lady Carleton was one of the foremost hostesses in Bath. She presided over many events during the season, from formal dinners and dances to picnic parties and musicales.

Miss Heywood nodded. "They're old friends of my grandfather, the Earl of Gordon. Their ball promises to be a grand affair."

"I would expect nothing less," James replied. "Your brother is escorting you?"

"He is." She hesitated for a long moment. "Will you be staying long in Bath?"

He looked at her, frowning. "That depends."

"On what, sir?" she asked.

James didn't answer.

Chapter Two

"**M**iss Heywood?" Miss Winthrop stood from her chair at the small table in the corner of Molland's. A dark-haired girl with a solemn countenance, she was soberly and unostentatiously dressed in a round-brimmed bonnet and a gown of toffee brown wool. The light through the mullioned window glinted on the gold frames of her spectacles.

Any unease Hannah had felt entering the busy pastry shop receded at the sight of her long-time correspondent. She came forward to meet her through the crowd, the heavy skirts of her day dress brushing against people as she passed.

Hannah's newly appointed lady's maid, Ernsby, followed in her wake. At home Hannah had been accustomed to looking after herself, but such independent ways wouldn't serve in Bath. Here, she must take care to observe every propriety. There could be no more outings unaccompanied. No more dressing herself or arranging her own hair. Her parents had hired Ernsby for that purpose. A superior-minded sort of creature, well-schooled in the rigors of her position, she had traveled down with them from Heywood House in the servants' carriage.

"Miss Winthrop?" Hannah queried with a tentative smile. "How do you do?"

"Very well, thank you." Miss Winthrop curtsied. "I'm pleased to meet you at last."

Hannah curtsied in return. "And I you. I so rarely have the opportunity to meet my correspondents face to face."

"Nor do I. Most of mine live in London or Paris or even America. I've long resigned myself that we shall never cross paths in person." Miss Winthrop gestured to the table by the window. "Shall we sit down? We've much to discuss."

Hannah took a seat. Outside the window, Milsom Street was still damp from this morning's rain. Ladies and gentlemen in heavy cloaks and overcoats stepped over the puddles, undeterred, to visit the fashionable shops that lined the street.

It was doubtless the reason why Molland's was so busy; everyone having dropped in to take the chill off. Hannah's own pink cashmere pelisse remained buttoned to her chin as she drew her chair up to the table. She had brought a shawl as well, along with an umbrella, not willing to risk catching cold so close to her debut. She placed them on the seat beside her.

Ernsby settled herself nearby, availing herself of a cup of tea while Hannah and Miss Winthrop ordered for themselves.

"It's a laudable undertaking," Hannah said sometime later, after they'd been warmed by their tea and had dispensed with the necessary pleasantries. "I've thought so from the first, but..." She flipped through the pages of the slim journal that Miss Winthrop had paid a local printer to produce, examining the essays and illustrations with building admiration. "I hadn't any idea it would look so impressive."

Miss Winthrop beamed. "I aim for the *Animal Advocate* to be as well regarded as any journal produced by a traditional publisher."

"It seems to me you've succeeded." Turning another page, Hannah found her article on the benefit of horses to a person's health and happiness. It was a short piece, not more than five hundred words, included among dozens of other essays, poems, and short stories written by animal welfare advocates. Among them, none of the authors were identified by gender. Only their first initial and surname were used. Hannah's piece was attributed to H. Heywood.

Looking at it, she felt a swell of pride. "I've never seen my words in print before. Not with my real name attached to them."

Miss Winthrop leaned across the table to examine the essay along with Hannah. "I hope I've done them justice."

"Indeed, you have. They appear ever so much more commanding here than they did when I set them down with my quill."

"Print has that effect. The only difficulty lies in establishing our authority for making such claims. A gentleman's journal would cite the author's full name and credentials. Whereas we ladies must strive to maintain our anonymity. Absent that, many of us dare not speak freely without risk of being labeled dangerous eccentrics."

Hannah's mouth compressed in a disapproving frown. "I refuse to believe that compassion can ever be equated to eccentricity."

"But you *must* believe it, Miss Heywood. You of all

people. A young lady making her debut can't be too careful. *I* know. My own come out was tainted by gossip about my peculiarity."

Hannah didn't know anything about Miss Winthrop's personal history, other than that she was the daughter of a clergyman in the nearby village of Locksmore. Their letters had largely been limited to the subject of animal welfare. "Did you make your debut in Bath?" she asked.

"Two years ago," Miss Winthrop admitted grimly. "Had I the ability to go backward in time, I'd never have done it. It was a dreadful experience, and—as my father says—far too costly for so little return." She paused for a moment before explaining, "I'm told that I talked too much on serious subjects, and was altogether too opinionated for people's comfort. I'm also an abysmal dancer, which meant I served no purpose at parties, not even to make up numbers. By the close of my season, all the invitations had completely dried up."

"I'm sincerely sorry to hear it," Hannah said. "Social events are trying at the best of times. I know too well how easily things can all go wrong."

Miss Winthrop pushed her spectacles further up on her nose. "Some of us are ill-suited for fashionable society. Both by aspect and by nature. I don't refine on it too much. My attentions are better served elsewhere."

"The journal does you credit." Hannah resumed turning the pages. At the end of the thin publication, there were several small sketches of animals—two dogs, a cat, and even a donkey. The latter was distinguished by one white ear and one white fetlock. The words **Lost or Stolen** were emblazoned above. "Are these—?"

"Reports of animals who have gone missing in the West

Country. That one is Sweet William, a girl's pet donkey taken from Fallkirk's Farm six months ago in Bidbury, a village outside of Saltford. The *Animal Advocate* hasn't a large list of subscribers at present, but it will help to get the word out. Perhaps he and the other missing pets can be found."

"Poor little dears," Hannah murmured. She couldn't imagine the pain of losing one of her own pets. "When will you send out the first issue?"

"It went out in the post this morning. I'll send the rest as orders come in."

"I look forward to receiving my copy."

"Take that one," Miss Winthrop said. "I have others at home."

Hannah accepted it gratefully. "Have you given any thought to your next issue?"

"Oh yes. If all goes to plan, the journal will go out monthly. I've already begun accepting contributions for the May issue."

"You are ambitious," Hannah said. "I admire you for it."

"It is in a worthy cause." Drawing on her gloves, Miss Winthrop moved to stand. "Perhaps we might meet again?"

"Assuredly." Hannah stood, gathering the journal, her umbrella, and shawl. "Not all of my hours will be consumed by balls and assemblies during my visit. I shall have ample time for my friends."

Miss Winthrop smiled. "I should like to call you friend, Miss Heywood."

"Hannah, please."

"Mattie," Miss Winthrop replied, returning the courtesy. "Shall I call on you in Camden Place?"

"Please, do," Hannah said. "My parents are arriving this afternoon with the remainder of the servants, and my horse and dogs, so it may be a bit busy for company, but anytime tomorrow or the next day would be convenient, I'm sure."

After taking her leave from her new friend, Hannah returned to her family's rented house in Camden Place, along with her maid. She and Ernsby entered to find the hall crowded with packing cases and trunks.

"Your parents have just arrived, Miss Heywood," Mrs. Pritchett said.

Hannah quickly divested herself of her bonnet, gloves, and pelisse. She handed them to Ernsby. "Where are they?"

"Your father is in the library with your brother," Mrs. Pritchett replied, "and your mother is in her room, unpacking. She has your dogs with her."

"Thank you," Hannah said, heading for the stairs.

By *her* room, she understood the housekeeper to mean *their* room. The choice of words was a matter of delicacy. Most fashionable couples didn't share a bedchamber. Hannah's parents had always been an exception. They shared a room just as they shared every other aspect of their lives. It was a scandalous fact to some of the servants. To Hannah, it was an example for her own future marriage.

She ascended the steps to the third floor, her skirts clutched in her hands. The master's chamber was located at the end of a floral-carpeted corridor. She rapped softly on the door. The faint sound was answered by the high-pitched barking of Evangeline and Tippo.

"Come in!" her mother called in answer. "But pray don't let them out!"

Hannah slipped into the room, shutting the door behind her. The grizzled pug and the three-legged black spaniel barreled toward her, wiggling with happiness. Hannah sank down on the floor, sweeping them up in her arms as they licked her face.

"You're all right, Evangeline," she said, kissing first one and then the other. "And you, Tippo, you foolish boy. I'm not going anywhere."

Hannah's mother, Phyllida Heywood, looked on with an expression of tender affection. A profoundly gentle lady, with dark auburn hair and a sweetly beautiful face, it was she who had taught Hannah to love and advocate for animals. Hannah couldn't recall her mother ever having been without an injured mongrel on the mend, not during all the years of Hannah's childhood.

Her mother's lady's maid, Gregson, stood beside the mahogany four-poster bed at the center of the room, single-mindedly unpacking a traveling case. There were trunks and boxes scattered over the mattress and on the upholstered chairs and small settee near the fireplace.

"They missed you dreadfully," Mama said as Hannah stood. "And so did I." She crossed the room to enfold her daughter in a warm, rose-scented embrace.

"It's only been one day and night, Mama," Hannah said, hugging her mother in return.

Her mother kissed her cheek before releasing her. "To Evangeline and Tippo, it has been an age. You were right to insist on us bringing them to Bath. I've been keeping them with me while Gregson and I unpack. A new house can be overwhelming to sensitive creatures. I advise accustoming them to it gradually."

"No fear," Hannah said. "I shall take charge of them now." She paused. "What of the other dogs?"

"Far happier at home," Mama said. "Flurry, Twig,

Ignatius, and Odysseus require familiar hearths and wide-open spaces. William and Sara will look after them in our absence."

Hannah nodded, satisfied with the answer. The Heywoods' married butler and housekeeper, William and Sara, had been with the family all of Hannah's life. There were no servants Hannah trusted more.

Her mother returned to the sarsnet-curtained bed where Gregson was removing a tissue-wrapped amber silk dress from the traveling case—a ball gown by the look of it. "Thank you, Gregson," she said. "If you would give us a moment?"

"Yes, ma'am." Setting aside the dress, the lady's maid dropped a curtsy before withdrawing into the dressing room.

"Is your father still with Charles?" Mama asked.

"In the library, Mrs. Pritchett said."

"Then we have time to talk." Mama sat down on the edge of the bed. She patted the place beside her. "Come. Sit with me a moment."

Hannah joined her mother, sinking down beside her on the mattress. Their full skirts bunched against each other.

Mama took Hannah's hand gently in both of hers. "Your brother tells me that Lord St. Clare called yesterday."

Hannah tensed. "Along with Kate, yes."

"And how do you feel about that, darling?"

Hannah's brow furrowed. She was used to sharing her thoughts and feelings with her parents. They had always treated her opinions with respect, never judging or ridiculing her, even when they must override one of her decisions for her own good. But confiding her feelings—such feelings that she had—about the cold, handsome viscount was a different matter. Hannah found herself unusually reticent.

"*Should* I feel something?" she asked.

"Your brother fears Lord St. Clare has developed a tendre for you."

Hannah was surprised into a laugh. The idea was too ludicrous to allow for any other reaction. "Indeed, he has not."

Her mother searched her eyes. "You're certain of that?"

Hannah's smile of amusement faded in the face of her mother's seriousness. She cast her mind back on the few interactions she'd had with Lord St. Clare, combing her memories for any sign of attraction on his part. There was nothing. Not a word. Not a look.

"He is civil," she allowed. "But I have never detected any particular warmth in his treatment of me."

"No," Mama murmured thoughtfully. "He is not, I suspect, a warm man."

Hannah looked at her mother. She knew her parents were very much in love. They took no pains to hide it. But Hannah's father wasn't a demonstrative man, for all that. He was solemn and reserved. Even grumpy, some might say if they didn't know him.

"Was Papa very warm to you when you first met him?" she asked her mother.

"Not warm, no. He is a serious gentleman, and at the time, prone to brooding. He had not long been back from the war. His thoughts were often turned inward. Still... I had a sense of him."

"You knew he was in love with you?"

"No, not then. I didn't know he loved me until after we married. But I knew he was my friend, and that my happiness was ever at the forefront of his mind. From the first, I felt safe with him."

Hannah compared her mother's description to her own overpowering feelings of shyness and discomfort whenever she was in Lord St. Clare's presence. There was no similarity at all. "I hope I shall have the same sense when I meet the gentleman I'm to marry."

"I pray you shall." Mama brushed a lock of Hannah's hair behind her ear. "If you don't, you must ask your father and me for our advice. We have experience on our side to guide you."

"You don't approve of Lord St. Clare?"

Mama was quiet a moment. "I have no reason to disapprove of him. When his family came to stay last month, he was all politeness. But I confess...I would prefer to see your fate joined to a gentleman of warmth and affection. One who values you exactly as you are, and who would not attempt to change you to suit his lofty standards."

"Lord St. Clare has never indicated a wish to change me. To be sure, he is in most every way a stranger. If not for Charles marrying Kate, I doubt I would have met him at all."

"But you have met him. And you are very beautiful, my dear," Mama said gently. "Some men see only that. They value outward appearance above all traits. It compels them to make inadvisable matches."

Hannah's brows lifted. *A match between her and Viscount St. Clare?* The prospect was too outlandish to contemplate. "Lord St. Clare has no interest in me. Not in that way."

She would know it if he had. She'd have felt it by now. Women *could* feel such things, couldn't they?

"And *your* interest?" her mother prompted.

"I have none. Not for him." Hannah gave her mother's hand a reassuring squeeze. "You're very sweet to worry, Mama, but you have no cause to. Whatever happens this season, I can promise you that Lord St. Clare is the last gentleman on earth I should ever choose to marry."

Chapter Three

The Carletons' stately house was located near the Abbey. Hannah had visited with her parents many times during their previous stays in Bath, but never during one of the elderly couple's famous balls.

She set her hand in her brother's as he assisted her down from the Heywoods' gleaming coach and four. It was a temperate evening, with no trace of the persistent rain that had plagued the city last week. The moon shone brilliantly in the star-spangled night sky. Along with the torches and lamplights, it reflected in the polished lacquer of the long line of carriages, illuminating the arriving guests in their elegant black-and-white eveningwear and lavish silk dresses.

Hannah's own ball gown had been ordered at the modiste during one of the many shopping excursions she'd made with her mother. Composed of white tulle over a white satin slip, it boasted short sleeves, a pointed waist, and full skirts trimmed in pink roses and three flounces of blonde lace. A matching lace bertha, fastened with another full-blown pink rose, lent a degree of modesty to her bare neck and shoulders. The bodice beneath was cut far lower than the evening gowns she'd worn in the country. It made her feel incredibly grown up.

It was meant to do so. Though she was already nineteen years of age, it was tonight that marked her true ascension to womanhood. Along with the ball itself, her gown announced that she was no longer a child. She was a lady ready to make a suitable marriage.

Hannah's parents followed them into the house, her father walking with the aid of his ebony cane. He was a tall, well-made man like her brother, with granite-hewn features and black hair liberally threaded with gray. Hannah's mother was at his side, her arm tucked in his, a perpetual source of support. The amber silk fabric of her ball gown shimmered as they passed the blazing candelabras that fringed the entry hall.

Lord and Lady Carleton waited there to welcome their guests. They were a distinguished, white-haired couple—his lordship portly and bewhiskered and her ladyship hawk-nosed and dripping with jewels. Behind them, a marble staircase curved up to the ballroom. Music floated down, along with laughter and the hum of animated conversation.

"Miss Heywood," Lady Carleton said. "You are a vision. Is she not, Carleton?"

"A fine-looking gal," Lord Carleton concurred jovially. "She'll have the pick of all the young bucks this evening, I wager."

Hannah's cheeks warmed. His lordship had a booming voice. Doubtless everyone in the receiving line had heard him.

Lady Carleton gave her husband a reproving tap with

her painted fan. "Hush, sir. You put the poor girl to the blush."

Hannah was glad when the elderly couple turned their attention to Charles and her parents. While they briefly conversed, she cast an uneasy glance up the stairs toward the ballroom. There were reputed to be more than two hundred guests attending this evening. Most of them would be strangers to her, and not all of them kind.

A pulse of anxiety throbbed at her throat.

She swallowed it back. There was no reason to panic. She had her family with her. Not only her parents and Charles, but her future sister-in-law as well.

"Do you suppose Kate and her parents are already here?" Hannah asked her brother as he led her up the staircase. The music grew louder.

Charles bent his head, pitching his voice so she could hear him. "Lady Carleton said they arrived not ten minutes before us."

Hannah exhaled a breath of relief. "Thank goodness."

Together, they entered the crowded, candlelit ballroom. Hannah held tight to her brother's arm as they navigated their way through the crush. Guests were gathered in tight-knit groups over the polished wood floor, talking, laughing, and wafting their fans. A bank of crimson-curtained windows flanked the left end of the long, high-ceilinged room. At the right, the orchestra was assembled on a dais, playing an unobtrusive tune. The dancing hadn't yet begun.

"All right, dearest?" Mama whispered, touching Hannah's back as she and Papa joined them at the edge of the ballroom.

Hannah gave her a small nod. Her mother understood

better than anyone the struggle Hannah faced in combatting her shyness this evening. Mama was of a reticent disposition herself. It was she who had supervised the plans for Hannah's debut, every detail arranged to cause her daughter the least amount of distress.

But there was no alleviating the whole of Hannah's anxiety. Fear and agitation were, she suspected, an unavoidable fact of a young lady's launch into society, regardless of her disposition. So much hinged on the success of one's first ball. If all went right, a young lady would be firmly set on the path toward a brilliant season and—God willing—a brilliant match. But if all went wrong...

Before Hannah could dwell too much on her chances of failure, her dire musings were mercifully interrupted by Kate and her parents.

John Beresford, Earl of Allendale, was a commanding gentleman, tall and handsome with silver-streaked golden hair and the same cool gray gaze as his eldest son. His much-adored countess, Margaret, was on his arm. She was a petite lady, possessed of striking beauty and an enviable confidence of manner.

They greeted Hannah's parents warmly. The two families had met several times since Charles's and Kate's engagement and enjoyed a certain degree of familiarity. While they exchanged pleasantries, Kate rushed forward to clasp Hannah's hand.

She was a copy of her famously beautiful mother—mink-haired and petite, with a delicate cleft in her chin. Her mazarine velvet ball gown matched the vivid blue of her eyes. "I've been looking out for you since we arrived," she said. "How are you?"

"A bit overwhelmed," Hannah confessed under her breath.

"You don't appear so. That's the important thing." Kate stepped back to admire Hannah's toilette. "How well your gown has come out! And you chose the pink roses instead of the red, I'm pleased to see."

"Mama procured them this morning."

"You look lovely, my dear," Lady Allendale said, turning her attention to Hannah. "It's no wonder your parents are glowing with pride."

Hannah's mother and father smiled at her. Hannah managed a small smile in return, not wanting to disappoint them.

"Lady Carleton has chosen a polonaise for the first set," Kate said. She glanced at the paper fan dangling from Hannah's wrist. "Is that your dance card?"

"It is." Hannah showed it to her. "Charles has put himself down for a country dance."

Kate flashed an arch look at her future husband. "How chivalrous of him."

Charles smiled. "One does one's best."

"You may rely on Ivo for a dance as well," Kate said. "He's here somewhere with his betrothed, Miss Burton-Smythe. My brother James might have stood up with you too, if he'd troubled to come."

Hannah gave Kate an alert glance. "He's not attending?"

"Not that I'm aware," Kate answered.

A bewildering mixture of relief and disappointment flooded through Hannah. She didn't let it show. She was too conscious of everyone's attention on her face. Not only her mother, father, and brother, but Lord and Lady Allendale too.

Were they all as curious about Hannah and Lord St. Clare as Hannah's mother had been? And all because Lord St. Clare had so inexplicably come to Bath?

Well, Hannah thought stoutly, this would surely set their suspicions to rest. For if Lord St. Clare had any romantic interest in her, he would have been here tonight to stake his claim. Instead, he hadn't come at all.

It was difficult not to take it as a slight.

Still, Hannah supposed it wasn't wholly a surprise. Lord St. Clare had called at Camden Place but twice since his visit on the day of their arrival. Both times, it had been in the presence of their families. Hannah had exchanged hardly any words with him, her shyness in his presence having only increased after her mother had suggested that he might have a tendre for her.

"It's no great loss," Kate said. "You don't want to be spending all of the evening dancing with present and future relations. What you require is an eligible gentleman." She looked to the others. "If you will allow us to take a turn about the room?"

Hannah's mother inclined her head. "By all means."

Kate linked her arm with Hannah's. "Walk with me," she said, drawing Hannah away. "Your father and brother are too imposing, that's the trouble. Few gentlemen will dare approach you with them looming nearby."

Hannah felt several curious looks in her direction, both from ladies and from gentlemen, as she strolled the perimeter of the ballroom with Kate. Her stomach trembled under their scrutiny. It was difficult to be stared at, whatever the circumstances. One never knew if those staring were being critical or admiring.

"A respectable gentleman must seek permission from my parents before asking me to dance, mustn't he?" she asked.

"No, indeed," Kate said. "Not unless he's a very dull dog. You don't want one of those. As for the other gentlemen, it's not disrespectful for them to ask you directly. It's only a waltz or a polka, after all, not a proposal of marriage. One needn't involve one's father in the transaction."

"But if we're not acquainted—"

"Any gentlemen interested in dancing with you will apply to our hosts for an introduction. That's why I suggested we take a turn. You want to be seen. A lady is always at her best when she's in motion."

They hadn't been promenading long when Lady Carleton intercepted them. She had a gentleman with her, just as Kate had predicted.

"Miss Heywood! There you are. And Lady Kate. How charming. May I present Sir George Dacres of Middlebury Hall as a very worthy partner?" Her ladyship urged the gentleman forward. "Sir George? Miss Heywood, granddaughter of the Earl of Gordon, and this is Lady Kate Beresford, daughter of the Earl and Countess of Allendale."

"Miss Heywood. My lady." Sir George bowed to them. He was a man of moderate height, with a neatly trimmed beard and side-whiskers. Not an unbecoming figure of a fellow, but nowhere near as devastatingly handsome as a man like Viscount St. Clare.

Which was nothing to the point. Hannah shouldn't be comparing gentlemen to Lord St. Clare as though he was the secret standard of her heart. She wasn't looking for a man with a striking appearance. She wanted one with an admirable character.

Perhaps Sir George might be him?

He offered his hand to her as the orchestra struck up the music for the opening march. "If you would do me the honor?"

Hannah mutely accepted his offer, allowing him to lead her onto the floor.

The other couples took their places, while those who weren't dancing receded to the edges of the ballroom to watch.

Any shyness Hannah felt at dancing with a stranger was promptly overshadowed by the focus it took to remember the sinking steps and turns of the polonaise. She found herself looking down at her feet far more than she ought, only to raise her gaze and realize that she'd forgotten her place. It made conversation difficult. On every occasion Sir George attempted to engage her, she could only reply by saying yes or no—that is, when she remembered to reply at all.

By the time the polonaise came to a close, Hannah had dispensed with any idea that Sir George might be the one for her. Plainly impatient with her awkwardness, he was all-too eager to search out a different partner.

Lady Carleton was undeterred. She introduced Hannah to a succession of other gentlemen as the evening progressed—younger sons of the gentry, country squires, and a widowed baronet.

Hannah danced with them all to similar effect. Indeed, there wasn't a single set she was obliged to sit out for lack of a partner. Charles and Ivo were the only ones among them who made the effort enjoyable. With them, at least, she lost some of her anxiousness and could actually take pleasure in dancing. As for the rest of the gentlemen...

They were all of them civil, and many of them kind, but none were in any way romantic.

Hannah finished a country dance with her latest partner, a self-important young baron from Dorset with an impeccably groomed mustache. He led her back to her parents as the other guests assembled for the next set. It was to be the first waltz of the evening. It was also the supper dance. Whoever partnered her for it would have the privilege of dining with her.

Thus far, the waltz had remained unclaimed on her dance card. Hannah anticipated Lady Carleton would supply her with a partner for it just as she'd done the other dances. But as Hannah approached her parents, it wasn't her ladyship she spied standing with them along the edge of the ballroom.

It was Lord St. Clare.

Chapter Four

James had been invited to the Carletons' ball along with the rest of his family. He hadn't planned on attending. He'd already indulged his unwilling attraction to Hannah Heywood far more than was good for him.

By rights, he should have left Bath days ago. He should have returned to Worth House or to Beasley Park. Better yet, he should have traveled to London. It was there among the beau monde where he would find the bride best suited to his future plans. A lady who would aid him in rehabilitating the Beresford name, not add a further complication to his efforts.

But James hadn't done any of those things. He'd remained in Bath, brooding over his conflicted feelings with increasing aggravation.

He wasn't generally an indecisive man. In the past, he'd always known his own mind. Decisions had come easily to him, every choice made to advance his goals and further his familial ambitions. He'd never felt himself at odds with a course he'd chosen. And he'd certainly never had to rationalize a bad choice to suit his own selfish desires.

The act of doing so left a sour feeling in his stomach. But there was no favorable alternative. Not when his attraction to Miss Heywood was affecting his mood, his work, and even his sleep.

Having made up his mind, James summoned his faithful valet, Smith, to help him change.

A short time later, James arrived at the Carletons' house, his muscles tight with a bitter resolve. A buoyant country dance was playing when he entered the ballroom. The ball was already half over. The candles in the two large chandeliers had burned low, and the air was redolent with the fragrance of beeswax floor polish, perspiration, and eau de cologne.

As luck would have it, it was James's younger brother, Ivo, who first spied his arrival.

"You dratted scoundrel," he said, approaching James with a smile. "Must you always be so disobliging? That's twenty pounds I'm out."

James arched a supercilious brow at his brother.

Ivo came to a halt in front of him. Like all the Beresford males, he was possessed of fair hair and gray eyes, with a tall, athletic figure. "Kate wagered me that you'd appear before the supper dance. I bet that you'd come afterward, if you came at all."

"The supper dance is next, I take it," James said, unamused by his brother and sister's antics.

"A waltz." Ivo's eyes danced with gleeful humor behind his spectacles. "Shall I direct you to Miss Heywood's parents?"

James didn't rise to his younger sibling's bait. It wasn't

the first time Ivo had nettled him about Miss Heywood. James had, initially, strenuously objected to Ivo's courtship of Meg Burton-Smythe. Ivo naturally took great pleasure at the prospect of James abandoning his long-held principles for what he perceived as an equally unsuitable young lady.

"That won't be necessary," James said coolly. He cast his gaze over the room, finding Captain Heywood and his wife seated near the bank of windows. They appeared to be watching the dancing.

"Miss Heywood isn't with them," Ivo informed him, as though James hadn't eyes enough to see for himself. "She's danced every set since the opening polonaise. Lord Fennick is partnering her for this one." He shot a mischievous glance toward the dancers. "A handsome devil if I say so myself."

James stiffened. He knew Lord Fennick. They had been at Oxford together. They hadn't been friends then, or even friendly. Exactly the opposite. Fennick had frequently made sly, mocking references to the Beresford family's scandalous history, perpetually trying—and failing—to provoke James to anger.

Fennick had also been instrumental in getting James blackballed from the university's informal boxing club. It had been a well-aimed blow, considering James's skill at the sport. One that Fennick had loudly attributed to the purported questionableness of James's pedigree.

Following his brother's gaze, James found his former rival at the end of the long line of dancers, wearing the same oily smile and equally oily mustache he'd worn at school. Miss Heywood was positioned across from him. Clad in a white, rose-trimmed ball gown, she was smiling shyly up at her partner as he turned her in a wide circle before they separated and resumed their place in the line. The delicate flounces of lace at her bosom and hem fluttered as she moved.

James's chest tightened. He was struck anew by the inherent quietness and grace in her person. She was lovely, of course. But it wasn't that which had beguiled him so thoroughly against his will—against his self-interest and his reason. It was the softness in her. The tender gravity in her gaze, and the reticence in her manner.

He had been pursued all his life. From boyhood, girls had been throwing their handkerchiefs at him. He'd long become adept at avoiding all efforts to entrap him into matrimony. But Miss Heywood hadn't made any attempts in that vein. Quite the reverse. She often took pains to evade his company.

As he looked at her, James experienced a rare, and totally unfamiliar flicker of masculine insecurity. What if it wasn't only shyness that made her behave as she did toward him? What if she simply didn't like him?

The music swelled as the country dance neared its end.

Dismissing his doubts, James headed toward Miss Heywood's parents.

Ivo followed him for a few steps. "Good lord. You really came for her sake, didn't you?"

James flashed his brother an arctic glare. "Have you nothing better to do?"

"What could be better than this?" Ivo wondered. "But have no fear. I won't spoil your air of frozen dignity. I shall enjoy my triumph from afar until Meg returns from the ladies' retiring room."

"She has my sympathies," James muttered.

Ivo grinned. "And now I've provoked you to spite. This evening gets better and better."

James strode on, privately grateful when Ivo had the decency to give up his pursuit. To James's siblings, everything was a lark. They had no sense of decorum. If the future of the family were left to them, the Beresford name would soon be synonymous with folly.

He made his way through the crowd, nodding at passing acquaintances, but not stopping until he reached the Heywoods.

On catching sight of him, Mrs. Heywood murmured something to her husband. Captain Heywood's already stern expression seemed to grow sterner still. He and his wife rose from their seats.

"Captain. Mrs. Heywood." James bowed.

"Lord St. Clare." Captain Heywood bowed in return. He was a serious gentleman, with graying black hair and the same military bearing as his son. An honorable gentleman too, by James's reckoning.

"My lord." Mrs. Heywood inclined her head. She possessed the same air of quiet reserve as her daughter, but there was no shyness about her. She looked James directly in the eye. "I didn't realize you would be attending this evening."

"I had not anticipated being free," James replied. "By happy chance, I found myself at liberty."

"A happy chance indeed," Mrs. Heywood said.

With a flourish of strings, the country dance came to a close. The couples dispersed from the floor, gentlemen leading ladies back to their parents and friends. Lord Fennick emerged through the crowd with Miss Heywood on his arm. Her gaze at once alighted on James. An expression of astonishment passed over her face.

"Miss Heywood." James sketched her a bow as she came to join them.

Her eyes were very wide. "Lord St. Clare." She curtsied.

Lord Fennick exchanged a bow with James. "St. Clare."

"Fennick," James said.

Fennick's mouth curled in a sneering smile as he looked at James. But he didn't prolong the encounter. He thanked Miss Heywood for the dance and then, bowing once again to her and her parents, promptly took his leave.

Miss Heywood scarcely seemed to register his departure. She was staring at James.

"Forgive my tardiness," he said to her. "I was unavoidably detained."

"But I didn't—" She faltered. "That is, I-I wasn't expecting you."

James couldn't tell if his absence had been noted with any degree of regret on her part. He sincerely hoped it hadn't. Though his indecision had been justified, and his reluctance to commit himself well-merited, he had no desire to hurt her. "I trust I'm not too late to claim the next dance?"

Miss Heywood exchanged an uncertain look with her parents before answering. "It's the supper dance, my lord. And...it's a waltz."

"Ah," he said. "I'm not tardy after all, it seems. Indeed, it appears I'm right on time." He offered her his hand. "If you would do me the honor?"

Miss Heywood's cheeks pinkened. She slowly slipped her hand into his. "I thank you, yes."

James felt a surge of satisfaction. She may not be the right young lady for him, but the moment felt right nonetheless. He was determined to make the most of it.

Hannah's heart fluttered wildly as Lord St. Clare led her out onto the polished wood dance floor. He drew her through the crowd, away from her parents and any interested friends or relations, not stopping until they'd reached the opposite end of the ballroom.

Horns and strings swelled to life as the orchestra commenced the first chords of a dramatic waltz. Hannah recognized the piece. It was a popular composition by the Austrian composer Joseph Lanner. She had the music for it at home, along with several other of her favorite of Lanner's waltzes.

The couples surrounding them stepped into each other's arms with well-practiced elegance.

Lord St. Clare turned to face Hannah, his gloved hand still holding hers.

Looking up at him, a surge of shyness went through her, worse than any she'd felt since arriving at the Carletons'. She'd never seen him in full evening dress before. The crisp white necktie, white waistcoat, and flawlessly cut black suit set off his tall, broad-shouldered frame to magnificent effect, amplifying his already daunting handsomeness to an uncomfortable degree.

She had previously had difficulty meeting his eyes, but now... How was she to face such golden splendor with even a semblance of composure? The effort to keep her countenance—

His arm circled her waist, strong and certain, making her breath catch in her throat.

For an instant, her mind went blank. She had to prompt herself to set her hand on his shoulder in return. It was firm as granite under her fingers, with no trace of padding. His commanding figure owed nothing to a tailor's art. He was a sportsman like the rest of his family, his leisure time taken up with riding, fencing, and boxing.

Drawing her closer against him, he effortlessly spun her into the first turn.

Hannah sucked in another sharp breath.

It had been months since they'd waltzed together at Beasley Park. She'd forgotten how it felt to be held by him. The heat. The decisiveness. The lean, muscular power.

Her pulse raced as he guided her across the floor. Many of the older generation still considered the waltz a scandalous dance. It necessitated the partners being in a closed hold, which some likened to embracing on the dance floor. Hannah had never credited the comparison while practicing with her dancing master, or with her brother. But when Lord St. Clare was her partner, she felt the similarity all too keenly.

If he was feeling it too, he didn't show it. He gazed down at her, his expression as inscrutable as ever. They danced in silence for several moments before he spoke. "My brother informs me that your debut has been a great success."

"I don't know about that, sir," she replied breathlessly.

"He claims you've danced every set."

"I have," she acknowledged. "Though never twice with the same gentleman. I fear I'm not a very congenial partner."

"No? I find you quite congenial." His arm tightened around her waist holding her closer. Her rose-festooned skirts swirled about his legs. "See how well we fit together?"

Hannah's heart quickened. "It's owing to *your* mastery of the dance, not to mine."

"You are too humble, Miss Heywood."

A thrill went through her as he waltzed her around the room. Dancers twirled past them, swooping and turning, but Hannah paid them no mind. The music was humming in her veins, her feet following Lord St. Clare's lead as naturally as if they'd been practicing together.

She looked up at him in wonder. "How easy you make it seem."

"A waltz shouldn't be difficult."

"It isn't with you."

The hard lines of his face softened a fraction. "I shall take that as a compliment."

She gripped his shoulder as they made another sweeping turn. A smile curved her lips. She'd never known dancing with a man could be so exhilarating. And that it should be so with him! A gentleman who usually made her too nervous to keep her thoughts in order, let alone her steps.

"I didn't think you would be here this evening," she confessed.

"I've been remiss," Lord St. Clare said. "I should have made my intentions plain."

"You've doubtless been busy." Though she couldn't imagine with what. His reasons for remaining in Bath were a mystery to her. Aside from Ivo's engagement, there was nothing to keep him here.

Unless Hannah's mother had been right.

Her words echoed at the back of Hannah's mind. *Your brother fears Lord St. Clare has developed a tendre for you.*

53

A tendre.

Hannah still couldn't believe it. And yet...

And yet, he had come tonight. Not just to dance with her, but to partner her in the waltz.

"You have your brother's wedding to Miss Burton-Smythe to think of," Hannah continued when the silence had stretched too long. "And Kate's wedding to Charles too." She gave him another faint smile. "We shall soon be family, you and I. Brother and sister, practically."

He looked back at her, unsmiling. "Not quite brother and sister."

Warmth suffused Hannah's midsection. He seemed so serious. She could almost believe he did feel something for her other than the civility one might owe to the sister of his future brother-in-law.

It was a dangerous prospect. Tonight, when she was alone in her room with her dogs, Hannah might allow herself to entertain it. But not here. Not while they were dancing, at least. It would be a sure recipe for a stumble.

She lapsed into silence again, letting him guide her as the other dancers waltzed past and the music flowed over them. All the while, he gazed down, giving her the full force of his attention. Her cheeks heated under the intensity of it.

"My lord, I—"

"James," he said.

She blinked in surprise. Her head shook reflexively. "Oh, but I couldn't."

"You address my brothers by their given names, do you not?"

"Well...yes. But Ivo and Jack aren't..." She fumbled for the words to explain.

Ivo and Jack were boys to her. Teasing, merry-hearted

brothers. While Lord St. Clare was in every way a man. And not a brother or any other kind of relation, but a handsome, unattainable gentleman so perfect that, most times, he didn't seem entirely human.

"I would be gratified if you bestowed me with the same honor," he said.

Hannah could think of no polite way to refuse. "If you insist." She gave him a disgruntled glance. "But I must say it feels like an unforgiveable liberty."

His mouth quirked faintly. "Am I so above your touch?"

"Not just mine," she said candidly. "Everyone's." She paused. "You may call me by my given name if you wish it."

"I very much wish it," he said. "Hannah."

The butterflies in her stomach fluttered their wings with increased vigor. Rarely had anyone spoken her name with such husky inflection. She wondered if she'd imagined it?

He spun her in another turn, waltzing her down the length of the floor. Hannah caught a fleeting glance of her mother and father standing at the side of the ballroom. They weren't alone. Lord and Lady Allendale were with them.

Hannah felt a flicker of self-consciousness. "They're all watching us."

James cast a glance at their parents before returning his attention to Hannah's face. "Not only us. Charles and Kate, and Ivo and Miss Burton-Smythe are dancing as well."

"Are they? I haven't seen them." Hannah turned her head to look for the others only to lose track of her steps. She nearly trod on James's foot. "Oh! I do beg your pardon!"

"Keep your eyes on mine," he said.

Her gaze jerked to his in apology. "I'm not usually so clumsy."

"You're not clumsy at all."

"Not so long as I let you lead," she said, chagrined.

"Then let me," he said. "I won't steer you wrong."

Chapter Five

"It was admittedly not the great success I'd hoped it would be," Hannah said as she walked Evangeline and Tippo along the green across from Camden Place. "But taken altogether, I cannot be disappointed."

Mattie Winthrop strolled at Hannah's side, a patterned shawl twined about her arms. "It's over now, at any rate," she replied sensibly. "The other events you attend won't be half so unnerving."

"I pray they won't," Hannah said.

Last night's ball had been enough of a trial on its own. She'd hated being so much on display, and had quailed at meeting new people. It was a grim foreshadowing of her season to come—endless months of balls and assemblies and unrelenting awkwardness.

Of course, it hadn't been *all* bad.

She'd taken great pleasure in the music, and she had largely enjoyed the dancing. But the purpose of it hadn't come close to being fulfilled. None of the gentlemen she'd partnered with had resembled the kind, warm-hearted future-husband she'd envisioned for herself. Among them, only Lord St. Clare had sparked a flicker of romance in her soul.

But not Lord St. Clare anymore. He was James.

James.

After waltzing with her, he had escorted Hannah to the candlelit dining room for supper. There, they'd shared a meal together. It hadn't been an intimate one. Their families had joined them at the table—her parents, Lord and Lady Allendale, Charles and Kate, and Ivo and Miss Burton-Smythe too. The mood had been merry, the conversation animated, and the privacy nonexistent.

James had left immediately afterward.

At the time, Hannah had owned to a feeling of disappointment. She had thought his presence might mean something. That he would remain until the ball ended, asking her to dance another set with him, or perhaps taking her for a walk in the garden.

But he hadn't done any of those things.

Hannah had finished out the ball just as she'd begun it, dancing and socializing with a succession of polite strangers. She'd stayed until the end, returning to Camden Place with Charles in the early hours of the morning, exhausted in body and spirit. On waking at midday, she had still felt the lingering effects of her disappointment, but she hadn't indulged them. She had her dogs to tend to.

They walked ahead of her at the end of their leads, Tippo prancing on his four legs, and Evangeline hopping on her three.

"Have you any engagements today?" Mattie asked.

"None. Though I must return home before receiving hours. There may well be callers."

"There often are the day after a ball, especially if one has proved popular."

"I don't know about popular," Hannah said, "but I did meet several new people."

"Did any of them seem likely to support the cause?"

Hannah frowned. "There was no opportunity to inquire. Not while dancing." A gust of wind over the green whipped at the rose satin ribbons of her bonnet. She brushed them back from her face. "But if anyone should call today, I will make sure to ask them."

Mattie drew her shawl more firmly about her shoulders. "It would be wise to do so. You wouldn't wish to wed a gentleman who isn't in accord with your philosophies."

Hannah doubted there were any marriage proposals in her immediate future. Not after what could only be described as a lackluster debut.

It was some relief that she hadn't done anything to distinguish herself in a negative light. But neither had she emerged as the belle of the ball. She'd been too quiet and timid to dazzle anyone. And she certainly hadn't been dazzled in return. Not unless one counted James's brief appearance.

She only hoped that future events during her season would draw a wider array of gentlemen. Perhaps then she might stand a chance of meeting a man whose thoughts and opinions aligned with her own.

"Speaking of my philosophies…" She guided the dogs back toward Camden Place. "I was considering writing an essay on the importance of feeding one's cats."

Mattie flashed her an interested glance. "As opposed to…?"

"Wrongly presuming they'll hunt for their supper.

Many cats won't—or can't. If more people understood their obligation of care, we may have fewer hungry cats roaming the street."

"Some of those cats are the products of abandonment," Mattie said. "It is the common way when people travel to another of their houses for the season. Many are accustomed to leaving their cats behind, untended. They imagine the cats will look after themselves until they return."

"Unforgivably foolish," Hannah murmured.

"Ignorance is to blame," Mattie said. "The trick is to educate without scolding."

"My essay wouldn't scold. I would simply explain the realities, and offer suggestions on how compassionate people might mitigate them."

"You would be writing for publication?"

"For your next issue of the *Animal Advocate*, if it isn't too late."

Mattie smiled. The front door of the Heywoods' house in Camden Place was just ahead. "I'm honored that you wish to contribute another piece."

"Then you'll accept it?"

"Send it to me when you've written it," Mattie said. "We can discuss it then."

Heartened, Hannah bid goodbye to her friend, before returning to the house. She let the dogs off their leads in the hall.

Mrs. Pritchett hurried to meet her. "You have a caller, Miss Heywood," she said in a low voice as she took Hannah's bonnet, gloves, and pelisse.

Hannah glanced at the case clock in the corner. Receiving hours hadn't commenced yet. "So early?"

Her mother had gone shopping with Lady Kate and Lady Allendale this morning. Hannah didn't expect her back before one.

"Who is it, Mrs. Pritchett?" she asked.

"It's Lord St. Clare," the housekeeper answered.

Hannah started. "And he's come to see...*me?*"

"He has, miss. He's just speaking with your father now, if you'd like to take a moment to refresh yourself?"

Hannah smoothed an anxious hand over her windblown hair. "I suppose I'd better." Evangeline and Tippo milled about her skirts, their nails clacking on the marble floor. "Would you please take the dogs down to the kitchens? They'll be wanting their luncheon."

"Very good, miss." Mrs. Pritchett herded the dogs through the door that led to the servants' stairs.

Hannah raced up to her room where she quickly put herself in order, washing her face and hands, and then—with Ernsby's assistance—repairing her hair and changing into a fresh gown. When she'd finished, she went straight to the drawing room only to find it empty. Perhaps Lord St. Clare was speaking with Papa in his library? She was just debating the propriety of joining them there when James entered the room.

Her already quivering pulse leapt with apprehension. She stood from her place on the sofa.

James bowed before coming to join her. He was dressed in an impeccably cut dark coat, shawl-collared vest, and light-colored trousers. His jaw appeared freshly shaven and his fair hair was combed into meticulous order. It shone with a subtle application of pomade, making the darker threads of blond gleam like burnished gold in the sunlight that filtered through the drawing room windows.

Had Hannah been looking for a flaw in his person, she couldn't have found it. Every inch of him was in perfect order.

She glanced past him. "Is my father not with you?"

"He sent me ahead." James motioned to the sofa. There was a vague agitation about his manner. "Will you sit down?"

"Yes, of course." Hannah resumed her seat, folding her hands in her lap. She waited for him to sit, but he did not.

He paced to the fireplace, standing there a moment in silence before turning and, resolutely, walking back to the sofa. He sat down beside her.

Close beside her.

Hannah felt his knee brush hers through the layers of her petticoats and horsehair crinoline. Her breath stopped, only to come out all at once in a tumbling rush of speech. "My mother isn't here. She is out with your mother, I believe, and your sister. They've gone shopping."

"So I understand."

"I might have gone with them, but I had arranged to take a walk with my friend, Miss Winthrop. She lives very near here." Hannah paused only long enough to draw breath to continue. "She's the publisher of the *Animal Advocate*, the new animal journal I mentioned to you at Beasley Park. The one that printed my article on the benefits of horses."

"Yes, I recall." His gaze was intent on her face. "Miss Heywood." His voice deepened. "Hannah."

"Yes?" Her own voice came out unusually thin and high pitched.

"It has been sometime since I've begun to think of you in terms that are—"

"Oh, you needn't—"

"May I speak?" he asked her. "Your father has given his permission."

Hannah's hands clenched tighter in her lap. Her palms dampened and her pulse pounded in her ears. She understood all at once that her mother and brother had been right. James must have a *tendre* for her. He must have come to Bath for her, and to the ball last night for her, and now he was here today, after first speaking to her father. But not just speaking to him. Gaining his *permission*.

It could all only mean one thing.

She wasn't at all prepared for it. "Yes, but truly, you—"

"I own that I have struggled with my feelings," he said. "You are not, it is to be admitted, the sort of young lady I had anticipated attaching myself to. However, since almost the first moment of our acquaintance, I have found myself unable to fix my attentions on anyone else. I admire you greatly, despite my justifiable misgivings, and believe that, with effort and mutual endeavor, we would ultimately do well together. I beg you would accept my proposal of marriage."

Hannah stared at him blankly. She had no experience of marriage proposals, but surely they were meant to be more romantic than *that*?

He'd said nothing of love. Nothing even of affection. He'd admitted to struggling over his feelings rather than welcoming them. To having 'justifiable misgivings.' It was an insult, though not, she suspected, an intentional one. The sting was no less sharp. She felt it in her soul.

A bleak future materialized before her, as vivid as a waking dream. She could, at once, see it all quite clearly. Were she to accept him, he would always find her wanting.

He would see only her flaws, her failures. He would never appreciate her strengths. It would not be long before he regretted having ever proposed to her. By then it would be too late. They would be stuck with each other, both of them miserable.

It wasn't what she wanted. No matter that she'd been nurturing something like a school-girlish affection for him. That the mere sight of him provoked butterflies in her stomach. It wasn't enough. She wanted more. Indeed, she deserved more.

Gathering her courage, she made her answer. It didn't come easily. Though she knew the polite order of words, she was not practiced at refusing. "I thank you for your attentions," she said with what she hoped was a creditable degree of calm. "I'm very sensible of the honor you do me. But no. Thank you. I do not wish to marry you."

James's handsome face betrayed an almost imperceptible flinch. "You're refusing me?"

Hannah's stomach quivered. Good gracious, she was, wasn't she? "I believe I must."

"Why must you?"

"I don't belong in your world, sir."

"I should think that *I* am the best judge of that."

"And you have indeed judged it so. You admit yourself that you've struggled. That you've had misgivings."

"Not about your character, or about the basic suitability—the admiration that I—" He broke off, seeming to collect himself. A muscle pulsed in his cheek. "My doubts have been confined to your ability to move in fashionable society. Part of my life must naturally be in town. Your shyness won't serve you there. You will have to develop confidence to succeed in London."

"I don't wish to move in London society."

"I shall guide you," he assured her. "I'm confident you'll rise to the challenge."

"Guide me," she repeated.

"It worked well for us when we danced together."

Hannah shook her head. She recognized his intentions were well meant. Even so, he didn't understand. "Marriage isn't a waltz," she said. "It's a partnership. I don't desire to be led. And I don't desire to change into something I'm not. When I marry, it will be to a gentleman who values me as I am."

His jaw tightened. "I see I'm to be punished for my honesty."

"No. Indeed, I hope we shall remain friends. We are soon to be—"

"Brother and sister, yes. So you've said." He stood abruptly. His face was hard, his expression wiped clean of emotion. "If that is your final word, then I must respect it." He gave her a stiff bow. "Miss Heywood." He turned to leave.

Hannah rose swiftly before he could quit the room. "*James.*"

He stopped by the drawing room door, his back to her. His broad shoulders were taut beneath the line of his coat.

She took a hasty step toward him only to come to halt. "I do like you very much," she said softly. "I-I wish my answer could have been otherwise."

He remained where he stood a moment longer before striding out of the room.

Chapter Six

Hannah returned to her seat on the sofa, her throat tight with emotion. She'd never received a proposal of marriage before. And she certainly hadn't anticipated receiving one from James Beresford, Viscount St. Clare. She hadn't even known he admired her until he'd said so.

But admiration wasn't love.

She hadn't done wrong to refuse his offer. They were ill-suited; their visions for the future too disparate to guarantee any chance of happiness for either of them. It had been a kindness really, telling him no. Even so...

She rather felt as if she was going to cry.

"Hannah?" Her father entered the drawing room, balancing some of his weight on his ebony cane. The injury he'd suffered to his right leg while serving as a cavalry captain in the Peninsular Wars necessitated the use of it. "Is Lord St. Clare—"

"Gone," she said bleakly.

Her father exhibited no surprise as he came to sit beside

her on the sofa. He leaned his cane next to him. "I had anticipated he might be."

"Did he apply to you for—"

"He did."

Hannah couldn't imagine what *that* scene might have been like. Her father was a former soldier, and not generally warm in his dealings with others. His kindness and gentleness were reserved for his family alone. "What did you say to him?" she asked.

"That the decision was yours to make."

She gave her father a wretched look. "How do you know I've made the right one?"

Papa set a reassuring hand on her back. "Your mother and I have confidence in you, sweetheart."

Her eyes stung with the threat of tears. "I refused him."

Papa's expression was solemn. "I had anticipated that as well."

"I fear I hurt him."

"He'll recover."

"You didn't see his face." Hannah recalled the way James had looked after he'd risen from the sofa. "He made himself vulnerable to me and I injured his pride."

Her father rubbed her back. "You've done him a service," he said. "Some men benefit from being knocked down a peg. It's character building."

"I'd no idea of knocking him down. I only said that I shouldn't like to have to change in order to be accepted."

Papa's brows lowered. "Did he ask you to change?"

"He requires a wife who can move in London society. A lady who will be successful there. He thought that, with an effort—" Hannah stopped herself. "But that isn't what I want."

"What do you want, pet?"

She gave him a faint, rueful smile. "A marriage like yours and Mama's, of course."

Papa's stern countenance softened at the mere mention of her mother. "Ah. Something to aspire to, indeed."

"Will you tell her about Lord St. Clare's visit when she returns?"

"I will."

"She will be shocked."

"No. That she won't be," Papa said. "What she will be is even prouder of you than she already is."

"Proud? Because I rejected the heir to an earldom?"

"Because you listened to your heart."

"I don't know," Hannah said. "It's aching awfully at the moment."

"There will be other proposals," her father promised her. "Better ones. Soon, that ache you feel will be but a distant memory."

Hannah found the thought of future marriage proposals cold comfort after what had just passed. As for her heart, she sincerely hoped her father was right.

JAMES WALKED THE STREETS OF BATH FOR OVER AN hour, his emotions in turmoil. He was stunned. Hurt. Perhaps even angry, though whether at Hannah Heywood or himself he couldn't tell.

When he thought of it, he couldn't even remember quitting the Heywoods' house. He had no recollection of retrieving his hat and gloves from the footman, or of departing from Camden Place. It was only Hannah's words that remained.

I do not wish to marry you.

Of all the eventualities James had accounted for, an outright rejection hadn't been one of them.

His pride was to blame. He'd been so certain of being accepted.

Though perhaps not entirely certain.

When he'd entered the drawing room and seen her there, looking so quiet and self-contained, an unaccountable tremor of doubt had assailed him. It was that which was to blame for his botching his proposal. If he had, indeed, botched it.

Again, he couldn't quite remember.

He thought he had spoken to her frankly, acknowledging the obstacles, but asserting his belief that together they could overcome them. He'd told her that he admired her, hadn't he? That he thought only of her?"

James raked a hand through his hair in frustration.

"Marriage isn't a waltz," she'd said. *"I don't desire to be led. When I marry, it will be to a gentleman who values me as I am."*

An acrid sensation took root in James's chest. He *had* botched it, hadn't he? He'd implied he didn't value her. That he didn't want her for his partner.

And yet, he couldn't shake the unhappy suspicion that she'd have refused him regardless. From the moment he'd sat down beside her in her parents' drawing room, she'd been pulling away from him, attempting to stop him from saying what he'd come to say.

He felt like a prize fool.

By the time he returned to his family's house near the

Circus, receiving hours had begun. The sound of feminine laughter drifted down the stairs, punctuated by Ivo's deep baritone voice.

James was in no mood to join his family in entertaining afternoon callers. Passing his hat and gloves to an obliging footman, he crossed the hall, heading for the billiard room. He'd nearly reached it when his father's voice sounded behind him.

"James," he said. "Back at last?"

James grudgingly came to a halt. He turned to face his father. "As you see."

Lord Allendale was dressed for home in tweed trousers and a loose-fitting sack coat. He stopped outside the doors to the library. "And how was Miss Heywood?"

James wasn't generally surprised by his father's prescience. This time, however, it gave him a decided jolt. "What makes you think I saw her?"

"Aside from the fact that you unexpectedly appeared at a ball last night, where you waltzed with her and dined with her, and then left without dancing with a single other lady?" His father's smoke gray eyes glimmered with a flash of wry humor. "Nothing at all."

James suppressed a scowl. "If you already have the answers to your questions, why do you bother asking them?"

"I don't have the answers. I merely make assumptions based on what I know of my children—and on what I'd have done in the same circumstances." The earl opened the door to the library, gesturing for James to precede him inside.

James was in too foul a mood for conversation. He nevertheless obeyed his father's unspoken command.

Abandoning any idea he'd had of billiards, he stalked into the library.

His father followed him, shutting the door behind them. "You called on her, I presume."

James crossed the thick red and gold carpet to the tall shelves that lined the wall opposite. They were stocked with all the titles one might expect to find in a gentleman's library—great leatherbound tomes on history, philosophy, and geography. He absently scanned the spines. "Yes."

"Did you propose?"

"I did."

"And?"

James flashed his father a bitter glance over his shoulder. "She refused me."

Lord Allendale's brows lifted. This was plainly a turn of events he hadn't anticipated. "Did she?" he murmured to himself.

"In no uncertain terms." Turning, James leaned back against the bookshelves, folding his arms. The library stretched out before him, with its dark wood paneling, overstuffed chairs, and heavy red draperies. It smelled faintly of pipe tobacco.

His father regarded him from across the distance. "That explains why you look as though you'd swallowed poison," he said. "Sent you away with a flea in your ear, did she?"

James's jaw tightened reflexively. His relationship with his father had always been a good one. They rarely quarreled (except over what James had sometimes perceived as too much leniency afforded to his wild younger siblings). They also rarely talked with any degree of intimacy.

From childhood, James had been accustomed to

keeping his troubles to himself. He'd never wanted to add to his parents' burdens. Today was no different.

Except that his usually glacial control was at its lowest ebb. He'd been humbled. Robbed of his defenses.

"On the contrary," he said in the same bitter tone. "She told me that she likes me very much."

"Ah." The earl strolled to join him by the bookshelves. "But not enough, I discern."

James shrugged. "She prefers to marry a man who will accept her as she is."

His father shot him an unfathomable look. "Did you imply that you wouldn't?"

A dull heat crept up James's throat. It wasn't embarrassment. It was annoyance. And not at his father or Hannah. James was annoyed with himself. "I might have done," he said. "Inadvertently."

"It isn't like you to do anything inadvertently."

James made no reply. What could he say? That he'd made a thorough hash of it? That much must be evident already.

His father reached past him to withdraw a large book from the shelf. He tested the weight of it in his hand. "A history of Great Britain through the reign of James II," he said. "The last in a series of books my grandfather made me read when I was a lad, traveling with him in Italy. I never did finish it."

James's father had spent his formative years on the continent, being schooled by James's great-grandfather, the late Earl of Allendale. Travel, books, and a succession of eccentric private tutors had stood in lieu of Oxford or Cambridge. By the time James's father had returned to England, he'd been able to pass for a gentleman.

But only just.

There were few in fashionable society who had forgotten the ignominious circumstances of his birth. He'd begun life working in the stables at Beasley Park, the bastard offspring of a degenerate scullery maid and a legendary gentleman-turned-highwayman. It was only later that his legitimacy had been proven and he'd taken his rightful place as the heir to the earldom.

The rumors had nevertheless persisted.

James had been flayed by those rumors since he was a lad. He'd dealt with them daily when he was away at school, first spouted by boys and later by young men, like Fennick and the rest of his ilk. Men who wielded their flawless pedigrees like weapons against anyone they deemed a threat. Even now, when visiting London, there was always some loudmouth at James's club who—after dipping too deep—would spout off about the former stableboy who had become an earl.

It was the primary motive for James to marry well. The only remedy for the stain on the Beresfords' history was to link their family with another great house. One whose behavior, wealth, and pedigree were so unfailingly pristine that it would outweigh any hint of former scandal attached to the Beresford name.

That had been the plan, anyway, until he'd crossed paths with Hannah Heywood.

"I was determined that you and your brothers would do better than I did," the earl said. "Not a ramshackle upbringing, but a traditional one, befitting your station. Eton. Oxford. Respectable marriages into established, aristocratic families." He gave James a thoughtful frown. "As the eldest, I daresay you shouldered the bulk of that dream. It can't have been easy given the Beresford reputation."

"I haven't complained," James said.

"All the same..." The earl's frown deepened. "I believe I've asked too much of you."

James went rigid. Was his father implying that he hadn't been up to the challenge? That he'd failed in some way? "No more than is my duty," he said stiffly.

"Duty isn't the whole of a man's life. The very fact that you proposed to Miss Heywood tells me that you—"

"Miss Heywood has saved me from a great piece of folly," James said. "I was wrong to propose to her, especially now that Kate and Ivo have fallen short of the mark."

They had been expected to marry well too. Instead, Kate had betrothed herself to an ex-naval lieutenant and Ivo was engaged to the unpolished daughter of their family's oldest enemy, a vile country baronet. Both were a far cry from the aristocratic matches that had long been envisioned for them.

"You'd hoped to wed a lady of consequence," his father said. "We all know that." He tucked the book under his arm. "But the heart wants what it wants."

"I've said nothing of hearts."

"No," his father acknowledged. "You haven't."

James was silent. He wouldn't be sorry he'd approached his proposal to Miss Heywood logically, even if it had resulted in a refusal. He'd seen first-hand where unbridled passion got one. Every member of his family had lost their head at one time or another, going back generations. It was the very reason the Beresfords were in this predicament.

"Perhaps if you had," his father went on, "Miss Heywood might have—"

"There is nothing I could have said that would have persuaded her to accept me," James informed him. "That's the end of it."

"If you say it is, then it must be so." The earl smiled again as he turned to leave. "A pity. Particularly considering how assiduously you courted the girl."

The barb hit home.

This time James couldn't disguise the scowl that sank his brows.

He hadn't courted Hannah Heywood, it was true. He'd admired her yes, and he'd spent the past several months privately grappling with his attraction to her, but he'd made no outward show of it. Aside from a few dances, and the conversation they'd shared that night in the Beasley Park stables, there had been no intimacies between them. No sweet words. No lingering touches. No indication at all that he viewed her as anything more than a future relation by marriage.

When James had finally come to a decision in his own mind, he'd arrogantly assumed that would be enough. That Hannah would welcome his proposal. Instead, she'd had no warning of his intentions. His offer of marriage had taken her completely off her guard.

If he had it to do over again—

But he didn't.

Polite as it was, her refusal had been absolute. All that was left was for James to put this debacle behind him.

His feelings for her would surely fade with time. He would come to be grateful that he had escaped his brief moment of madness unscathed. Until then, there was only one thing to be done.

He would return to London.

Chapter Seven

Hannah learned that James had departed Bath quite by chance. It was Kate who revealed it. She was leaving Bath herself the following day, along with her parents, and had invited Hannah for an early morning gallop to say goodbye.

Riding in Bath wasn't the same as riding at home in the country. The cobblestone streets weren't well suited to horses. Most houses didn't even have an attached stable. The Heywoods' had been obliged to stable their own horses at an inn nearby. One of the grooms had brought Hannah's dappled gray mare, Jubilee, to her that morning, saddled and ready. Kate's groom had done the same, delivering her bay gelding, Ember, for her use.

The two young ladies had ridden out toward Lansdown where they'd enjoyed a gallop over the hills. The sun was shining and the sky was clear. It did much to boost Hannah's flagging spirits.

It had been several days since James's proposal and she

was still not quite herself. Try as she might, she hadn't been able to get his face out of her head. That look he'd had when she'd refused him. The way he'd flinched.

Hannah didn't regret rejecting his proposal, but she deeply regretted that she had caused him pain. It wasn't in her nature to hurt someone. Indeed, she hadn't imagined that James *could* be hurt. The realization that she had been the one to do it—that she'd had that power over him—had rattled her to her core.

She'd taken little enjoyment in her season in the days since. Not the dance at the Assembly Rooms, nor the dinner party she'd been invited to. She hadn't even been able to focus on writing her cat article for the *Animal Advocate*.

She was in perpetual dread of crossing paths with James again. And not because she was afraid of his reaction, but because she was worried about her own. Given what had happened between them, how on earth would she manage to look him in the eye?

Kate brought her gelding to a standstill at the top of the rise. She lifted her head to the sky, inhaling a deep breath of fresh air. "I shall miss this," she said.

"I shall miss you," Hannah replied, bringing Jubilee to a halt beside her. The gray mare tossed her head, objecting to the restraint. She far preferred galloping to standing still. "I wish you could stay longer."

"So do I," Kate said. "Alas, Bath will soon be sorely lacking in Beresfords. Ivo is to be the last of us, and he only for another few days. He's accompanying Meg and her father back to Letchford Hall on Saturday."

Hannah gave her an enquiring look. She wouldn't allow

herself to ask about James outright. She had no wish to betray a particular interest in him. As far as she knew, Kate wasn't aware of her older brother's proposal. No one was, except for Hannah's mother and father.

But all of Bath had seen him waltz with Hannah and sup with her at the ball. All were surely wondering if there was anything more to his behavior than mere civility to a young lady soon to be connected to him by marriage.

"James has already gone," Kate said in answer to Hannah's unspoken question. "He left the day after the Carletons' ball. Gone back to London, apparently. The insufferable fellow. I'd begun to think he might have a reason to stay, but..." Her brow creased. "As all my brothers do, he takes pleasure in thwarting me."

Hannah turned Jubilee in a circle to calm the mare's restlessness.

So, James had returned to London. And on the same day Hannah had refused his proposal. She supposed that was an end to it.

It should be a relief, really. Now she wouldn't have to see him again. Not until Kate and Charles's wedding, and that was months away.

But Hannah didn't feel very relieved. On the contrary. She felt the same lingering sense of regret she'd felt when she had refused him. He must have been badly hurt indeed to have left Bath so quickly.

"You're not disappointed, are you?" Kate asked.

"Disappointed? Me?" Hannah smiled. "Why should I be?"

"You must know we've been teasing James awfully about his reasons for coming to Bath. The truth of it is, I'd hoped he had come to court you."

Hannah bent her head, adjusting her gloved hands on her reins as Jubilee pranced beneath her. She made no reply.

Kate didn't require one. "I suppose, all along, it must have been this business with Ivo and Meg that brought James here. He didn't approve of their attachment initially."

Hannah had observed that much for herself when she and Charles had visited Beasley Park in January. Then, Meg Burton-Smythe had called unexpectedly during an after-dinner dance. The reception she had received from James and his family had been chilly at best. Understandably so, given the fact that Meg's father, Sir Frederick Burton-Smythe, and Lord Allendale were enemies of longstanding.

"He must have required further proof of Ivo's affections," Kate said. "Once assured, he had no more cause to remain. Nor why would he? James has no great fondness for Bath. He far prefers London. There were rumors last autumn that he might be courting Lady Augusta Newall, daughter of the Marquess of Deane. She's a paragon, apparently, as well as being highly connected. Perhaps he's returned to her?" She gave an absent pat to her gelding's gleaming neck. "Shall we ride back?"

Hannah numbly agreed that they should. The casual revelation that James had recently been pursuing someone else shouldn't matter to her. She had refused his offer, and there was an end to it. The information stung nonetheless.

A paragon, Kate had called the young lady.

A paragon.

Meanwhile, James had blithely referenced Hannah's failings even as he was professing his admiration for her. He'd spoken of struggling over his feelings. Of having misgivings.

It hurt far more to recall it than it had hurt in the actual moment. Then, she'd been too stunned to allow the words to properly penetrate. But not now.

She mutely turned Jubilee to follow Ember as Kate guided her gelding back toward town. Their respective grooms followed after them at a distance.

"James thinks only in terms of great alliances," Kate went on. "As though we Beresfords are pawns on a board, incapable of moving unless it's to advance some prestigious game."

Hannah rode up alongside her. The skirts of her close-fitting black wool riding habit fluttered in the breeze that gusted over the hills. "Has he always thought so?"

"He was encouraged in the belief by my great-grandfather. He had always dreamed that the family would regain its reputation. It was his son—my grandfather—who first submerged us in scandal. He was a known highwayman, you know. It's all rather shocking."

Hannah listened with unwilling attentiveness. She wished she weren't so eager to know more, but she couldn't seem to help herself. "A highwayman? Truly?"

"Oh, yes. He was a dreadful rogue. I never knew him myself. He died abroad, long before my parents married. Local people near Beasley Park still remember him, though. They still *talk*."

"One can't help who one's ancestors are."

"That's what Charles says."

"Charles knows?"

"I confessed it to him when the two of you visited Beasley. He did not seem troubled to hear it."

"Does it trouble *you*?" Hannah asked. "Having a family scandal in your past?"

"Not as much as it does James. Then again, he *is* the heir. It's he who must take the family into the future, not I." Kate flashed Hannah a sudden smile. "I shall soon be a Heywood, shan't I?"

Hannah smiled in return. "You certainly shall."

The following day, she bid goodbye to Kate and her parents. The day after that, Ivo and Meg Burton-Smythe departed, along with Meg's father, Sir Frederick. Hannah was left on her own in Bath with her parents and Charles.

This, it seemed was the real start of her season, not the brief illusion of romance she'd nurtured at the Carletons' ball. James was gone, probably returned to his pursuit of his London paragon. And Hannah was here, focused on her own future. An imperfect future, to be sure, but one that she hoped would ultimately be perfect for her.

<hr />

THE MARQUESS OF DEANE'S SPRAWLING HOUSE IN Mayfair boasted one of the grandest ballrooms in London. A trio of enormous imported crystal chandeliers hung from a domed ceiling that had been artfully painted to resemble the summer sky—all white clouds, shimmering sunlight, and flawless blue heavens. The guests gathered beneath it were no less illustrious. Noblemen and women of every rank were in attendance, each of them immaculately tailored, exquisitely coiffed, and dripping in jeweled cufflinks, diamond pins, and costly parures.

James crossed the crowded dance floor as the orchestra tuned up for another waltz. He had promised this one to Lady Augusta, the marquess's daughter.

The two of them had first met last year at a society dinner party. They had been seated beside each other at table. A pleasant enough experience.

It had occurred to James then that Lady Augusta possessed all the qualities he desired in a wife. He hadn't acted on the observation. Despite her inarguable perfections, she had failed to stir his interest. However, in the aftermath of Hannah Heywood's stinging rejection, James's thoughts had once again turned to the estimable Lady Augusta. Not eagerly, by any means, but with a certain sense of resignation.

Whatever tumult he felt in his heart, he was resolved to do his duty. There would be no more unplanned deviations from the course he'd set for his life.

"Lord St. Clare!" Another young lady hailed him as he passed. A delicate blond, fair of face and figure, she wore a lilac silk ball gown and three gleaming strands of amethysts.

It was Bertrice Paley, the sister of Silas Paley, one of James's classmates at Eton. James had once stayed with Silas's family during the school holidays. A tedious visit, during which Silas had peppered James with questions about the Beresford family's scandalous history.

James grudgingly stopped to acknowledge her. "Miss Paley." He bowed.

She curtsied briefly before batting him with her lace fan in mock displeasure. "I didn't know you were in London, sir. You might have called on my brother and me. We are both in town at present, with my father."

"How is Sir Andrew?" James asked. The baronet was afflicted with gout, an ailment from which he'd been suffering for many years.

"Poorly," Miss Paley said. "He remains at home this

evening. Indeed, he's threatening to leave London to take the waters. I have been attempting to dissuade him, but he insists we will depart within the week. It is most inconvenient."

"Please send him my regards."

"You may deliver them yourself, my lord, when you visit us." She dropped a calculating glance to her dance card. "Shall I put you down for a march?"

"I would be honored," James said. Taking his leave of Miss Paley, he walked on.

Up ahead, Lady Augusta was just leaving the floor, having completed a country dance on the arm of a duke's son. She murmured something to the young gentleman before detaching herself and moving toward James. "Lord St. Clare. I believe this waltz is yours."

James smiled. There was no warmth in it. He felt tonight just as he'd felt at every engagement he'd attended since returning to London—utterly empty. "I am come to claim it, my lady."

Lady Augusta smiled serenely in return. Her chestnut ringlets were caught up in pearl combs, revealing the swanlike grace of her long neck. She was an objectively beautiful young woman, in addition to her copious other charms. She had elegance in abundance. Confidence. Poise. Add to that, her wealth and pedigree, and it was plain why so many considered her to be the catch of the season.

She permitted James to lead her back onto the floor. They exchanged a bow and a curtsy as the orchestra struck up a waltz.

It was Strauss.

James recognized the melody as he stepped forward, taking Lady Augusta's right hand in his and setting his other hand at her waist. But it wasn't the melody he heard as he led her into the first swirling turn. His sullen heart overshadowed the music with quite another waltz. The Lanner waltz he'd danced with Hannah Heywood in Bath.

An aching swell of bitterness constricted his chest.

It took an effort not to succumb to it.

All his life, James had witnessed his parents all-consuming love for each other. It was an emotional anomaly, he'd believed. So rare as to be unattainable. Never once had he contemplated meeting a girl who would inspire such impassioned feelings within his own jaded soul. He had not thought it possible.

Until Hannah.

A young lady so beautiful and sweet, he'd known almost instantly, despite sense, despite strategy, that she was the one who had been waiting for him all along.

But it was impossible.

And not only because she wasn't right for him, but because she didn't want him.

Swallowing his bitterness, James refocused his attention on Lady Augusta. It was she who best suited his plans for the future. She was ideal in appearance, in behavior, in bloodline. And he felt...

Nothing.

The same nothing he'd felt on every other occasion he'd conversed with her, or danced with her, or taken her for a turn in a moonlit garden. She may be perfect for him on paper, but in reality, she fell entirely short of the mark.

He left the ball not long after dancing with her and Miss Paley, returning to his parents' townhouse in Grosvenor Square. He helped himself to a large glass of brandy in the drawing room and downed it one swallow.

After pouring himself another, he sank down in a wingchair by the cavernous fireplace, staring into the dwindling flames. He was still there, several hours—and several glasses of brandy—later, when his mother quietly entered the room.

She was wearing her flannel dressing gown, her thick mink hair arranged in its nighttime plait.

"What are you doing sitting here alone in the dark?" she asked.

"Drinking myself into a stupor," he answered flatly.

"Brooding, more like." Her slippered feet were silent on the thick carpet as she came to the fireplace. She stood over him a moment, her dark brows sunk in a measuring frown. "I've scarcely seen you since you arrived. You've spent every minute boxing, crossing foils with your fencing master, or dining at your club."

"I'm sorry I haven't been more attentive."

"I require no apology. I'd prefer an explanation."

"Father hasn't confided in you?" James huffed into his empty glass. "I'm amazed."

"Don't be impertinent," his mother said sternly. "You're not too old for me to box your ears." She drew closer to him. "Of course he's told me about Miss Heywood rejecting you. *And* about your belief that her refusal has saved you from making a grievous mistake."

James had forgotten he'd said that. Thinking of it now, he recognized the sentiment for what it was. Doubtless his father had recognized it too. It had been the very definition of sour grapes.

"What puzzles me is why you're behaving this way," his mother said. "You should be celebrating your happy escape, not pummeling hapless fellows at a boxing saloon."

"Not only boxing. I was at a ball this evening. It was at the Marquess of Deane's residence."

"I presume you saw Lady Augusta?"

"I did."

"After which you appear more despondent than ever." She studied his face. "Why, James?"

James gave his mother a bleak look. "I'm unhappy."

Her expression softened. "Oh, my poor love." She smoothed a rumpled lock of hair from his brow. "I know you are. But it's an unhappiness of your own making."

"Because I've fixed my heart on the wrong girl."

"Your heart," she murmured. "So, it *is* engaged?"

"What does it matter? She's not right for me."

His mother touched his cheek. "Right for you? Rubbish. Do you imagine your father was right for me?"

"You and father are soulmates. You've always said so."

"Yes, we are, but we made no sense otherwise. Not when we were your age. Our situations were too different and there were countless obstacles in our way. We had to fight to be together. Surely, I raised you to do the same." She tipped his chin up, compelling him to look her in the eye. "If you want her, my dear, *fight* for her."

"To what end? She doesn't want me."

"Is *that* what she said?"

James cast his mind back to those crushing moments after he'd proposed. *I do not wish to marry you*, she'd told him.

But that wasn't all she'd said.

Recalling the words Hannah had uttered as he'd turned to leave the room, James felt the faintest glimmer of hope.

"There," his mother said. "You see?" Bending over him, she pressed a brisk kiss to his forehead. "I'm going back to bed before your father comes searching for me. If you plan on setting off at first light, I'd advise you to do the same."

James bid his mother good night.

She was right.

Rising from his chair, he summoned his valet.

Chapter Eight

Hannah fastened her pink cashmere pelisse over her day dress. In the normal course of events, she would leave her letters in the hall to be collected by the postman. But the morning post had already come by the time she'd finished her cat article, and she was too impatient for Mattie to read it to wait until tomorrow.

"I shall take it to the post office myself," she informed her maid as she drew on her gloves. "Evangeline and Tippo will enjoy the walk."

Ernsby greeted this news with tightly compressed lips. She didn't approve of Hannah drawing attention to herself with her motley assortment of canines. "Perhaps if you had a handsome little spaniel or a prettily clipped poodle," the lady's maid had remarked on more than one occasion. "Then, you could parade them down the high street as much as you please. But this pair... they do you no credit, miss."

She nevertheless trudged dutifully behind Hannah and

her two dogs, away from Camden Place toward the post office in Broad Street.

Hannah had become more familiar with the city over the past week as she'd diligently applied herself to the business of her first season. Every day had been taken up with concerts, dinners, dances, and formal calls. What time she'd had left had been devoted to her animal interests. There had been precious few hours remaining to pine over icy blond viscounts.

Just as her father had predicted, the ache in Hannah's heart had gradually receded. In James's absence, there was nothing to remind her of what had caused it.

Neither was there any more favorable emotion to take its place.

None of the gentlemen Hannah had met since rejecting James's proposal had inspired any degree of interest in her.

But, as she often reminded herself, these were early days yet. There were many more weeks of entertainments to come. In the meanwhile, Hannah had plenty to keep her busy, both socially and intellectually.

She continued toward the post office with a purposeful step. It was less than a mile away. An easy enough distance for a country girl accustomed to tramping over the rolling hills of her parents' estate. Evangeline and Tippo trotted gamely at her side, sniffing at the air with interest as they passed horse riders and strolling pedestrians.

The population of the city was growing by the week, with newcomers arriving to take part in the season. Hannah felt the curious glances of some of them as she walked past. She doubtless provided quite a spectacle with her mismatched eyes and her three-legged dog. Even Tippo inspired a second look or two. He was an ancient pug, grizzled and bleary-eyed, though still quite happy to be out for a stroll.

They hadn't gone far down Broad Street when Hannah spied a costermonger's cart stopped ahead. There was a small donkey in its traces, its head hung low as the costermonger unloaded his wares.

Hannah cast a sympathetic look at the poor creature as she passed.

And then she looked again.

She came to a startled halt. "Good heavens!" she exclaimed under her breath. "That donkey has one white ear!"

"Indeed, miss," Ernsby acknowledged indifferently.

Hannah drew her maid aside as the balding costermonger continued unloading his crates of produce. Evangeline and Tippo milled restlessly around their skirts. "Sweet William, the missing donkey pictured in the *Animal Advocate*, had one white ear as well," she whispered. "And a white back fetlock too."

Ernsby's thin brows lifted. "Did he?"

Hannah peered at the donkey's muddy hooves. It was impossible to tell the color of his fetlocks. Not from this vantage point. Coming to an abrupt decision, she handed the dogs' leads to Ernsby. "Hold them a moment, if you please."

Before Ernsby could object, Hannah stepped down into the street. She walked around the donkey, examining it closely.

The costermonger paused in the middle of hefting another crate onto his shoulder. He was a rough-looking fellow in a course cloth coat, with a decided sneer about his mouth. "You looking for something, miss?"

A glimmer of white peeped above the mud on the donkey's back hoof.

Hannah stopped in triumph. "*That*," she said, pointing. "This donkey has a white back fetlock."

"What of it?" the costermonger asked.

"He matches the description of a donkey who was stolen from a farm in Bidbury last autumn."

The costermonger's already surly face darkened with anger. Letting his crate fall to the ground, he took a menacing step toward Hannah. "Are you calling me a thief?"

Ernsby made as if to join Hannah in the road, but the dogs had tangled their leads around her legs, preventing her movement. "Miss Heywood?" she called out in a shrill voice. "Perchance we should walk on?"

"I'm not accusing you of theft, sir," Hannah said to the man. "But this donkey *is* stolen, however you came into possession of him."

"Like hell he is. I bought him at the sales six months ago, fair and square."

Evangeline barked at the man's angry tone. Tippo gamely joined in. Several people strolling by slowed to look, curious about the cause of the commotion.

Hannah ignored both the dogs' barking and the interested glances of passing pedestrians. "In that case, the thief is very likely the person who sold him to you."

"Rubbish," the man spat.

"This donkey was taken from Fallkirk's Farm exactly six months ago. There's a sketch of him being circulated in a local journal. I've seen it myself."

"You don't know what you're talking about." The costermonger returned to his crate of produce. He bent to pick it up. "Be off with you. I've enough work to do without having to listen to hen-witted busybodies making nuisances of themselves."

Hannah positioned herself by the donkey's head. The little creature pressed his small, velvety nose against her hand in silent entreaty. It gave her all the courage she needed to continue. "You may say what you like about me," she replied to the man. "The fact remains, this donkey belongs to someone else."

The costermonger hoisted his crate back on his shoulder with a dismissive snort. "If you're not gone by the time I return, I'll be summoning the constable," he informed her. He turned to walk away.

Evangeline and Tippo continued barking at him as he went.

Hannah remained by the donkey, her shoulders squared and her back straight. "Summon him now," she said. "A constable is precisely the man we need."

Ernsby's face went pale. The only thing worse for a young lady's reputation than a public altercation in the street was an altercation involving the law. "Miss Heywood," she protested. "Surely you should not—"

"Aye, I'll summon a constable, miss," the costermonger growled, doubling back on Hannah. "I'll have you up on charges for interfering with my property." He reached out to grab her arm. "Now get away from that beast before I—"

"Before you what?" a cold, iron-backed voice interrupted.

Hannah looked up with a jolt, straight into the arctic gaze of James Beresford, Viscount St. Clare.

Chapter Nine

J ames brought his matched set of grays alongside the donkey cart. He'd only just returned from London. An arduous journey, the final length of which he'd made in his curricle, accompanied by his faithful tiger, Bill. They'd been driving toward the Beresfords' house near the Circus when James had seen Hannah Heywood in the street.

And not the shy, soft-spoken Hannah he'd parted from nearly two weeks ago, but a version of her he'd never seen before.

Gone was the blushing young miss unable to meet his eyes. The lady quarreling with the costermonger was standing straight and square, her eyes blazing and her voice commanding. She appeared in that moment entirely without fear. She also appeared rather magnificent.

"Ain't none of your business, sir," the costermonger replied to James. He again reached for Hannah's arm.

"Don't touch her," James said in a tone of dangerous calm.

The costermonger froze.

Giving an unspoken signal to his tiger to hold the horses' heads, James jumped down from his curricle. His hair was disheveled from the wind, his tan cord breeches and blue broadcloth coat dusty from the grime of the road. He paid his travel-worn appearance no mind. His attention was fully fixed on Hannah.

He strode to her side. "Are you all right?"

She stared at him for a moment in wide-eyed astonishment before collecting herself. "I'm perfectly well. It's this poor donkey who is in peril. He's a young lady's treasured pet, stolen from her family's farm last autumn. I recognized his markings at once."

"I didn't steal nothing," the costermonger snapped back. "I told the lass, I bought the little beast at the sales. Cost me fifteen shillings, he did. I've the proof of it at my lodgings."

"I'll give you a sovereign for him," James said.

Hannah started. "Oh, but you—"

"A gold sovereign?" The costermonger's eyes glittered. "I'll take it."

"Done," James said. He flipped the costermonger the coin. The man caught it in his fist. James called to his tiger. "Bill? Take this donkey back to my stables."

"Yes, Lord St. Clare," the tiger said.

The costermonger's eyes goggled to hear James's title. He scraped off his cloth cap and sketched James a clumsy bow. "Your lordship. Your generosity—"

"Miss Heywood." James offered his hand to Hannah. "Allow me to see you home."

Hannah looked from James to the costermonger and back again, as if she couldn't decide whether to be grateful for James's high-handedness or outraged by it.

James addressed her in a low voice pitched for her ears alone. "The less time we spend in the street, the less chance this unfortunate interaction will damage your reputation."

A flush of color rose in her cheeks. "Yes, of course." She set her hand lightly in his. "Ernsby? Will you—"

"I shall take your dogs back to Camden Place, Miss Heywood," the lady's maid said.

"Oh, no," Hannah replied. "They don't know you well enough yet. It would only distress them. I shall take them up with me." She glanced at James as he assisted her into his curricle. "If you don't object?"

"Not at all," James said. "I'll hand them up to you."

He waited only long enough to make sure she was settled on the high seat before turning to retrieve her dogs. He had met both of them last month at Heywood House. The three-legged spaniel was a shy creature. She cringed away as James gently gathered her into his arms. He passed her carefully to Hannah. "Here is Evangeline."

Hannah enfolded the dog in a reassuring embrace.

"And here is Tippo," James said. Unlike Evangeline, the ancient pug was happy to be held regardless of who it was doing the holding. He gave James's cheek a cheerful lick as James relinquished him to Hannah.

"Thank you," Hannah said. Her voice held a vague note of amazement. "I did not expect you would remember their names."

"Naturally, I remember." James vaulted back up into the seat. He took charge of the reins from Bill. The instant the tiger stood back from their heads, James gave the pair of grays the office to start. They surged forward at a brisk walk.

Hannah cast a final look back at the little donkey. Bill

was standing beside it as the costermonger unhitched it from its cart. Her lady's maid lingered nearby, staring anxiously after her mistress. "Poor Ernsby. She takes it all very personally. I do hope she won't hand in her notice."

James guided his team into the street. "Takes what personally?"

"Spectacle," Hannah said. "She was hired to safeguard my reputation. She'd rather not be obliged to witness me plunging it into infamy."

"I'd say you'd managed to avoid infamy for the moment," James replied. "But only just."

Hannah gathered her dogs closer. She bent her head to them. Her face was half hidden from James's view. "I thought you'd gone to London."

"I did," he said. "I've come back."

"Your family has already gone from Bath."

"I didn't return for them."

She fell quiet again.

James felt a flicker of uncertainty. Frowning, he expertly guided his team around a slow-moving carriage blocking their way. "I've never seen you as you were today," he said at length. "You looked..."

Perfect.

"I know how I must have looked," she acknowledged grimly. "I don't often consider the propriety of my actions when an animal's welfare is concerned."

"So I observed."

She stiffened. "I won't apologize for it. Had I not seized the moment, that donkey would have been gone. As it is—"

"He'll be safe in my stable within the hour."

"For which I am endlessly grateful," she said, sounding

rather formal. "I will, of course, repay you the gold sovereign you expended on the donkey's behalf."

"You owe me nothing."

"I can't guarantee you will receive reimbursement from the donkey's owner, Farmer Fallkirk. Though he and his daughter will certainly be pleased to see the little fellow. I shall arrange to return him to them without delay."

"*I* will take him to them," James said. "All you need do is relay their direction to me."

Again, she went quiet. And then: "You're offended by my behavior."

"I'm alarmed by it," James acknowledged. His blood simmered to recall the way the costermonger had reached for her. "That man was about to grab you."

"He didn't, thank goodness."

"If I hadn't arrived—"

"But you did," Hannah said quickly. "Indeed, your timing was impeccable."

"Miss Heywood—" He paused. "Hannah—"

"Yes, I know. You're quite appalled, aren't you? And no doubt thanking heaven that I didn't accept the offer you made me before you left for London."

James's hands tightened reflexively on the reins. He was amazed she would reference his proposal. But then, she seemed to have a knack for amazing him. Shy and timid as she was—

But she wasn't shy, was she? Not in the way people supposed. He'd had a glimpse of her true character that night in the Beasley Park stable. It had been the very thing that had first attracted him to her. And today he'd had more than a glimpse. The strength of her convictions had blazed forth, irrespective of the consequences, reminding him exactly why he'd abandoned London after less than a fortnight in order to return to Bath.

And to her.

"You presume to know all my thoughts," he said.

"No, indeed. But if you believed me unsuitable then, it stands to reason that you must recognize me as being doubly unsuitable now."

James slowed his horses. He'd reflected on the words he'd chosen for his proposal often during their time apart, and had swiftly come to regret them. "Did I say you were unsuitable?"

"Not in so many words."

"In any words?"

"You owned to having misgivings about my suitability, yes. *Justifiable* misgivings."

He inwardly flinched at the reminder. "It was ungentlemanly of me."

"But honest."

"Regardless, I shouldn't have said it. I hope that, one day, you can forgive me."

"There's nothing to forgive," she said.

He drove on, subsiding into silence. When the turning approached for Camden Place, he didn't take it. He continued along the main road.

Hannah didn't question his lapse. She had fallen quiet again too.

"How have you found your season in my absence?" he asked at last.

It was a damnable question. Naturally she would have met someone else. Several someones, in fact. All James had achieved by leaving Bath was to clear the field for them.

"Rather dull," she replied frankly.

Relief coursed through him. He didn't show it. He continued staring straight ahead, not betraying his delight at her pronouncement by so much as a twitch. "Dull, was it?"

"There was a dance at the Assembly Rooms. And, later in the week, a concert. And then—last evening—another dinner party. Thus far, the people have all been the same as attended the Carletons' ball."

"Not *all* the same," James said.

Color crept into her face as she glanced at him from beneath her lashes—the softest hint of pink. It was the same delicate shade as her cashmere pelisse. "No. Not all the same." There was an endless pause. "Why did you come back?"

"Because of something you said to me," he answered her.

Her gaze jerked to his. "*I?*"

"That morning when you refused my proposal, as I was leaving you, you said you wished your answer could have been otherwise."

Hannah stared at him.

James hesitated. She'd already refused him once. Had already told him that she wanted a husband with qualities he didn't possess. But the final words she'd spoken that day had been echoing in his head since he'd recollected them last night. It was those fateful words that had ultimately brought him to this very moment, here with the young lady who had uttered them so fatefully.

"Did you mean it?" he asked her.

⚜

HANNAH HELD EVANGELINE AND TIPPO CLOSE TO her as the curricle rolled over the cobblestones. She was grateful to have them with her. Absent their support, it would be just her and James alone. A daunting proposition! It was perilous enough as it was, seated so close beside him, listening to him talk about what she'd said to him in the moments after rejecting his proposal. She puzzled over what he could mean by it.

But there could only be one meaning.

He had come back to Bath, not for his family, but for her. He wanted to find out if he had any reason to hope.

She was fully aware of the implications of giving it to him. At the same time...

She couldn't bring herself to lie.

"Yes," she said. "I did mean it."

He cast her an unreadable look as the horses made another circuit down the road. He was obviously in no hurry to return her home. "*Could* it have been otherwise?"

"I daresay it could have," she allowed. "If the circumstances had been different."

"In other words, you can envision a set of circumstances under which you might have accepted me."

Hannah couldn't believe they were engaged in such a conversation. What could be served by it? "Possibly," she said. "If we're speaking of hypotheticals."

"Hypotheticals, then." He guided the horses past another carriage. "Perhaps if I'd made a greater effort to show you how well-suited we are."

"I cannot believe that we *are* well suited," she said. "Our personalities are so drastically dissimilar."

"Not *drastically* dissimilar. We're both loyal, honorable individuals who hold our families in high regard."

"Yes, but that—"

"We're principled people as well. And we don't deviate from those principles, regardless of how unpopular they might be."

She frowned. "Yes, I suppose."

"We take our responsibilities seriously."

"Certainly, but..." She hesitated. "You've said nothing of love."

"Love," he repeated.

"It's as important as any other principle. More important when one is speaking of matrimony. My own parents love each other deeply."

"As do mine."

"Then you allow that the emotion is necessary for a happy marriage?"

"I wouldn't say necessary. Many couples deal well enough together without the added burden of being in love."

Her brows lifted. "A burden, you call it?"

"It can be if it overrides rational thought."

Hannah couldn't conceal her disappointment at his bleak pronouncement. "I don't believe love is ever a burden." She paused, adding, "And it *is* necessary for me. When I marry, it will only be for love."

James's face was inscrutable. "And you don't love me, of course."

Heat flooded her cheeks. She could summon no reply. She hadn't anticipated him being so blunt.

"However, you did admit to liking me very much," he said. "Was that true?"

"Yes." She did like him. Rather too much, all things considered. He wasn't at all right for her, no matter that he was the only gentleman of her acquaintance to make her heart beat so swiftly.

"A strong liking might grow into love, given adequate inducement," he said.

"I expect it could, but…"

"But?"

"I would think it unlikely in this case. We are too different. We want different things of life."

"I want you," he said.

Her pulse quickened.

"All I ask is that you give me a chance to prove I'm worthy of your affections," he said. "If I fail, you may send me away again, and I'll trouble you no more."

"I didn't intend to send you away at all," she said in a rush. "I'd no idea you would leave Bath after I refused you. I was very sorry you did."

"No sorrier than I," he replied with uncommon gruffness. "I hadn't been in London above two days before I realized what a mistake it was."

"I'm glad you came back."

His gaze flashed to hers. "Are you?"

"If you hadn't appeared when you did, I'd have had to summon a constable to deal with that costermonger. It would have been an awful spectacle."

His mouth hitched with wry humor. "Is it only my assistance with recovering purloined pet donkeys that makes you glad of my return?"

She shyly returned his glance. "No," she said. "Not only that."

His eyes betrayed a flicker of warmth. "Do you give me reason to hope?"

Hannah's heart thumped hard. If she were wise, she

would rebuff him again. She had plenty of valid reasons to do so. He wasn't sweet enough. Gentle enough. Romantic enough.

But what if he could be?

What if, beneath all that icy sternness and formality was a man to whom she might safely entrust her heart?

It was surely too small a chance to pin her future on, but in these cases, a lady had to go with her instincts. And every instinct in Hannah was whispering only one answer.

"Yes," she said.

Chapter Ten

It wasn't until Hannah entered Camden Place that she realized she had failed to ask James about his pursuit of his London paragon. She had also entirely forgotten to post her cat article to Mattie Winthrop. The folded pages were still safely tucked in her embroidered reticule, the urgency of them all but forgotten in the face of Hannah's encounter with James.

Once he had obtained her assurance that there might still be a chance for them, he had promptly returned her to her parents' house. Hannah had been grateful for it. Their candid conversation had quite stolen her breath away. She didn't think she could have managed another word on the subject of love, courtship, or marriage—not even a hypothetical one. And she certainly couldn't have summoned the nerve to broach the topic of Lady Augusta. By rights, Hannah shouldn't even know about the lady, let alone be questioning James about her.

As it was, Hannah had a dreadful time dissuading him

from accompanying her inside. He'd wanted to pay his respects to her parents in person, everything proper and above board. Hannah had ultimately convinced him not to, insisting it was better if she spoke to her mother and father first.

Mama appeared in the entry hall within seconds of one of the footmen admitting Hannah and her dogs into the house. Concern etched her brow. "Ernsby told us what happened," she said. "Are you quite all right, my dear?"

"Yes, indeed." Hannah unleashed Evangeline and Tippo. The two dogs gave her mother a cursory greeting before trotting off toward the kitchen stairs. "Lord St. Clare nicely resolved the issue. He purchased the donkey from the costermonger." She removed her bonnet and gloves, passing them to the waiting footman with a murmured word of thanks. "Although, I really don't think he should have done, not if it was the costermonger who had stolen the donkey in the first place. But it *was* the most efficient course, I must say. His lordship has promised to drive the little creature to Fallkirk's Farm tomorrow and personally return him to his family."

Her mother's face registered a flicker of impatience. "I wasn't thinking about the donkey. I was thinking about *you.*"

Hannah's father was not far behind her mother. His cane clacked loudly on the tiles as he came to join them. His expression was even sterner than usual. He scanned Hannah as though checking for damage.

"She's unharmed, my love," Mama reassured him.

Hannah experienced a surge of guilt. "I didn't mean to worry you both. I'm sorry if I did."

Mama drew Hannah from the hall, away from the servants, and into the privacy of a small, simply furnished anteroom. Papa accompanied them, closing the door behind him.

Hannah looked between her parents with building anxiety. "Are you very cross?" she asked. "I know I should not have created a public spectacle by confronting that costermonger, but you must allow that, given the circumstances—"

"We're not cross, sweetheart," Papa said. "Only concerned."

Mama ran her hand over Hannah's arm in a gentle pass. "Ernsby told us that Lord St. Clare took you up in his curricle."

"Oh, yes. He was very kind. He sends his compliments to you and Papa, by the way."

Her parents exchanged a glance.

"That is very civil of him," Mama said. "I only wonder what he's doing back in Bath when all his family has gone. He's not pressing his case, is he?"

Papa surveyed Hannah's face. Whatever he saw there answered the question before Hannah could answer it herself. "Of course he is," he said. "Only a fool would have abandoned the field so soon. Something I suspect the viscount realized the instant he'd returned to London."

"She's already refused him," Mama replied. "It isn't gentlemanly for him to persist."

"He hasn't done anything untoward," Hannah said, coming to James's defense. "To be sure, Mama, he was exceedingly polite. He merely asked if I meant something I'd said to him the day I declined his offer. He wondered if he had cause to hope."

"Which you've given him?" Papa asked.

"I have," Hannah admitted.

Mama was visibly flustered by this news. Papa moved closer to her, setting a hand at her waist.

"It's her choice, love," he said.

"And our duty to advise her," Mama replied to him. She turned her attention back to Hannah. "You find him outwardly pleasing, I don't doubt. And, given the generosity of your heart, you hope he might become the kind of gentleman you would be willing to marry. But a man doesn't change his character, dearest."

"I don't expect him to change his character," Hannah said. "My hope is that, given time, he'll reveal it." She made an effort to explain what she didn't fully understand herself. "I have been in his company so little since we met. We scarcely know each other at all. And he isn't an easy man to know, I confess. But perhaps, given time..."

"You are an optimist," her father said. "Like your mother. Always seeing the heart of gold beneath the gruff exterior—in humans *and* animals."

"A cold exterior is a very different thing than a gruff one, Arthur," Mama returned.

"I don't believe him cold," Hannah said. "He's merely... controlled."

"Controlled," Mama repeated dubiously.

"In any event," Hannah continued, "I've given him leave to court me. He has even promised to take me with him tomorrow when he returns the donkey to Fallkirk's Farm."

Her father's brows snapped together. "Now wait a moment. If he means to—"

"We will go in his curricle," Hannah said. "Riding in an

open carriage with a gentleman is perfectly unexceptionable, is it not? Even for a young lady making her debut?"

"Well, yes," Mama said. "But surely—"

"It's decided then." Hannah moved toward the door of the anteroom before her parents could offer another objection. "Forgive me, I must write to Miss Winthrop without delay. She'll want to know all the news about the donkey."

JAMES HADN'T ANTICIPATED GETTING A SECOND chance with Hannah Heywood. After setting her down in Camden Place, he headed for his family's house near the Circus, half convinced that his encounter with her had been the product of his imagination.

And it wasn't only the donkey, the costermonger, and the madcap mongrel dogs that had given the chance meeting an air of unreality. It was the way she'd felt sitting beside him in the curricle, so soft and shapely, with her full skirts billowing against his leg. The way she'd smelled—of clean herbal soap tinged with a hint of delicate rose perfume.

James had taken great pains not to say anything or do anything that might frighten her away. He had held back from expressing how sorry he was to have offended her. From begging her for a second chance.

But she'd given him that chance anyway—kindly, sweetly.

He was determined not to squander it.

James entered the kitchen. "Didn't expect you to be here, big brother."

"Nor I you." James drew out a chair. "What do you mean by it?"

"Nothing at all." Jack helped himself to another whole sausage. He had the appetite—and the dining habits—of a ravenous beast. "Thought the house would be empty, didn't I?"

James sat down. "You arrived this morning?"

"At three-odd, and somewhat worse for wear. I was imbibing with friends at that tavern near Beasley, when it occurred to me I should speak with Charles Heywood. I hired a chaise to bring me here straightaway. By the time I arrived, the drink had caught up with me and I promptly went to bed. Only just woke up half an hour ago."

"A charming tale," James said.

Jack flushed. "Well, you did ask."

"Why do you need to speak with Heywood?"

"He's a military man. A naval man, at any rate. I want his advice about something."

"Joining the Navy?" James suggested with no little sarcasm.

Jack's fork stilled halfway to his mouth. "And if I did?"

James stared at him in disbelief. "Good God. You're not serious?"

"Don't act as though the idea were completely insane. Most younger sons have commissions bought for them. We can't all be blessed with honorary titles, my lord Viscount St. Clare."

James had no sympathy for his brother's position. As far as James could see, it was he who had received the short end of the stick. The role of heir came with countless duties and obligations, many of them unpleasant. They weighed on a man. At times it could be difficult to bear. "Have you spoken to father about this?"

"No. I only just thought of it, as I said."

"You can *un*think of it, then. Our mother would never allow you to willingly put yourself in harm's way."

Jack's fork clattered to his plate. Irresponsible as he was, he hated being treated like a baby. It never failed to rub him on the raw. "I'm of age. The decision is mine to make."

"Not if you expect father to purchase you a commission it isn't."

Jack scowled. He pushed back from the table. "What are you doing here anyway? I thought you'd be in London paying court to that Marquess's daughter of yours. What was her name? Lady Amelia? Lady Arabella? Lady—"

"Lady Augusta," James supplied stiffly. "And I've never paid court to her."

"Let me guess," Jack said. "You've decided she's not good enough for you either."

"She's good enough," James said. "But she's not for me."

His brother was briefly diverted. "Aha. Someone has supplanted her, I see. And someone in Bath, as well." His face lit with sudden comprehension. "Not Hannah Heywood?"

James didn't dignify him with an answer.

Jack burst out laughing. "Oh, this is splendid! Does Ivo know? He must be crowing with glee. He said as how you'd fallen hard for her, but—"

"Are you quite finished?" James asked. He was beginning to grow irritated.

Jack stood from the table, still grinning. "What? Can't bear a little teasing on the subject? Too sensitive?"

James rose from his chair to face his brother. "I can bear a good deal from you and Ivo, but the moment I discover your juvenile japes have reached Miss Heywood's ears, you will find me strikingly absent humor."

Jack's smile faded.

It had been a long while since the Beresford brothers had lapsed into fisticuffs, but they had fought often as young boys—both in sport and in earnest. Their mother had constantly been called upon to nurse their black eyes, bloody noses, and split lips.

"You've too much Honeywell blood in you," she'd tell them as she swabbed their wounds. *"Try counting to ten, won't you?"*

"Or to one hundred," their father had advised. *"Beresford blood may be slower to boil than Honeywell blood, but it burns far longer. It will consume you if you let it."*

James had left all that behind him when he'd gone away to school. He'd mastered his Honeywell heritage, and his Beresford one too. But that double dose of multi-generational hot bloodedness was far from being dormant in his veins. It simmered within him like an underground river of molten lava, wanting only a necessary spark to set it off.

"I've no intention of causing insult to her," Jack said, on his dignity. "So, you can stop looking at me as though you're about to eviscerate me with your bare hands."

"I'm serious," James said.

"As I see." Jack frowned at him. "What are you worried about? Ladies from Plymouth to York have been falling over you since you were in leading strings. Why should Hannah be any different?"

"Because she is," James said. "Things are delicate. I'll not have you ruining my chances. They're precarious enough as it is."

Jack gave a snort of disbelief. "If you say so."

"I mean it, Jack."

"Well, then." His brother straightened his waistcoat. "I shall have to be on my best behavior, shan't I?"

Chapter Eleven

"It appears that St. Clare isn't the only Beresford in Bath," Charles said, reading the note one of the footmen had just delivered to him in the breakfast room.

Hannah regarded her brother from across the lace covered table in reluctant inquiry.

She had no great wish to discuss the Beresfords with him. Their family had already spent a good deal too much time on the subject for her comfort. Indeed, last evening at dinner, James's unexpected return had been the primary topic of conversation.

On rising this morning, Hannah had hoped they would have exhausted the matter. She'd been relieved to find only Charles at table, believing she might be allowed to eat her meal in peace.

Her brother took pity on her. "Jack is in town."

"Oh?"

Charles tucked the missive back into its envelope, laying

it beside his plate. "He invites me to join him for luncheon at York House this afternoon."

"I am surprised he isn't at Beasley Park or in London with his parents and sister."

"I'm not. He's young and restless, and very much surplus to requirements at the moment."

Hannah resumed buttering a triangle of toast. Tippo and Evangeline sat at her feet, half covered by the lace tablecloth, shamelessly begging for scraps. "I shall be happy to see him during his stay. I've not been in his company since he visited us at Heywood House."

"We shall have to make sure he's invited to some of the same entertainments," Charles said. "Young men of his age often find themselves at loose ends during the season. Better he join you at your dances and concerts than lapse into bad company."

"I'm sure James won't permit him to do so."

"*James,*" Charles repeated quietly.

The silver butter knife stilled in Hannah's hand. She lowered it slowly back to the table. "That *is* his name."

"His given name." Charles refilled his teacup from the silver pot on the table. "Did he invite you to use it?"

"Naturally, he did. It would be strange if I continued to address him by his title now that you and Kate are to be married. I don't, after all, address Ivo and Jack as Mr. Beresford, do I?"

"Neither Ivo nor Jack have proposed marriage to you," Charles said, refilling Hannah's cup in turn. "Not that I'm aware." He paused. "Unless you've been withholding that fact as well?"

Hannah gave her brother a speaking look. Charles hadn't learned about James's proposal until last evening.

He'd been annoyed that she and her parents hadn't confided in him earlier.

"I've not received any other proposals," she said. "As you're well aware."

"I had not thought you'd received the one." He set down the teapot. "More fool I."

Hannah broke off the crusts from her toast. She discreetly passed them to the dogs under the table. "You know why I didn't tell you."

"Because I'd have told Kate, and she'd have told Ivo, Jack, and her parents. Yes, so you've said. An excuse which fails to take into account the fact that I'm not in the habit of breaking family confidences."

Hannah dusted her fingers off on her white linen napkin. "Kate is soon to be your family. You would certainly have told her."

"Not if you didn't want me to."

Hannah smiled at her older brother's naivete. "Kate would have wheedled it out of you. You know she would have."

Charles gave an eloquent wince. He raised his teacup to his lips. "Perhaps you're right."

"I am." Hannah bit into the soft part of her toast. Beneath the tablecloth, the dogs resumed their begging, having already wolfed down their portion of the crust. "In any event, it scarcely mattered until yesterday. I had thought the matter quite over and done with."

"Had you confided in me, I might have warned you that it wasn't," Charles said. "A man like St. Clare doesn't give up easily."

Hannah's mouth dipped in a thoughtful frown. "Papa said something of the sort."

"He was right. And so was I when I warned our parents that St. Clare was developing an attraction for you."

She reached for her teacup. "I still don't know how you could have known *that*. I didn't even know it until he proposed. Just because he came to Bath—"

"It isn't only that," Charles said. "It's the way he looks at you. The same way he's looked at you since we visited Beasley Park."

Hannah's senses perked with interest. "What way?"

"As though he's trying to solve a puzzle."

Her spirits sank a trifle. She could guess what puzzle that was. "He doesn't want to like me."

Charles shook his head. "Hannah—"

"No, it's true. His brothers speak about it freely enough. So does Kate. James envisioned attaching himself to a paragon. He even has one in mind, I'm told."

"If he has," Charles said, "I've not heard of it."

"Kate mentioned her to me. She said she was a marquess's daughter, highly connected in London."

"St. Clare is here, not in London."

"I'm aware."

"It doesn't follow that you must grant him a second hearing," Charles said. "Say the word and I'll deal with him. He will trouble you no more."

"You're very chivalrous," Hannah said. "And very sweet. I'm grateful for it. And for Mama and Papa's advice and protection too. But this time..." She raised her teacup to her lips. "I do believe I shall handle things for myself."

Chapter Twelve

J ames arrived in Camden Place promptly at eleven to collect Hannah for their journey to Fallkirk's Farm. Captain and Mrs. Heywood welcomed him in the drawing room, both of them civil but reserved. Hannah stood next to them in her pink pelisse, straw bonnet, and gloves, looking a little anxious.

"It's less than three miles to Bidbury," Captain Heywood said. "It shouldn't take you above half an hour each way."

"Possibly longer with the donkey," James replied. "He's tied to the back of my curricle."

Hannah's face brightened. "How is he?"

"Exceedingly well," James said. "A warm mash and a night in a comfortable stable have worked wonders. You would hardly recognize him."

"Oh, I can't wait to see him," Hannah said. "He was so pitifully dispirited yesterday." She took a step toward the doors of the drawing room. "Should we—"

"Your tiger will be accompanying you?" Captain Heywood asked brusquely, interrupting his daughter.

Hannah came to a disgruntled halt.

"He will," James replied. "He's a capable hand with the horses."

"Curricles can be dangerous," Mrs. Heywood said. "I shall rely on you to bring my daughter back safely."

"I'm sure Lord St. Clare is an excellent driver, Mama," Hannah said.

"I won't let her come to harm," James assured Mrs. Heywood. "You may rely on me."

Captain Heywood looked at him steadily. "You and I will speak again when you return."

James solemnly returned his gaze. The last meeting he'd had with Hannah's father hadn't been a very encouraging one. In hindsight, James supposed that Captain Heywood had known how Hannah would respond to a proposal of marriage. The fact that James hadn't abandoned his suit after her rejection was likely cause for fatherly concern.

"I'm at your disposal, sir," he said.

Hannah gave her father a look of entreaty. "We should leave directly. Wouldn't you think so, Papa? The donkey is a little fellow and can't be made to trot too quickly."

"Naturally not," Captain Heywood said.

A short moment later, James was handing Hannah up into his waiting curricle. Bill was in his full livery for the occasion. He held the horses as they stamped with impatience. Even the donkey was twitching its tail, eager to be off. His head no longer drooped with resignation. His expression was alert, his eyes shining and his nose raised to the wind.

Hannah regarded the little beast with a smile of amazement. "You've had him groomed!"

"All credit to Bill." James climbed up beside her. "He had charge of him for the night."

"I'm obliged to you, Bill," Hannah said to the tiger. "He looks an entirely different animal."

Bill reddened. He was just a lad from the Beasley Park estate, scarcely ten years of age, and not accustomed to dealing with ladies. He muttered something about "just doing his duty" before retreating to his perch at the back of the curricle. From there, he could keep a close eye on the donkey as they traveled.

James started the horses.

Hannah pressed a hand to her bonnet as they surged forward. "The Fallkirks will be elated. I know I would be if one of my missing pets was returned to me unexpectedly."

"A happy circumstance that you encountered him as you did."

"Indeed, it was. To think, I nearly passed him without a second look. I was that focused on posting my article."

He gave her an interested glance as he drove the curricle. "What article?"

"A piece I'm contributing to the *Animal Advocate* on the importance of feeding one's cats. Many people don't feed them, you know. They presume a cat will hunt for their own supper. But not every cat is capable of hunting."

"That much I do know," James said. "My sister has two cats. I'm convinced they subsist on minced meat and cream."

Hannah smiled again. "Tabby and Major. I remember them well."

"Do you keep cats at Heywood House?" James asked. He couldn't recall seeing any outside the stables.

"Not in the house. It wouldn't be fair to them. Not with so many dogs in residence."

"How many dogs altogether?"

"Let me see." She appeared to perform a silent count in her head. "Six at the moment, not including the working dogs. Though that number is apt to change if the need arises."

"Do you anticipate keeping as many when you set up house of your own?"

She abruptly lowered her eyes.

James silently cursed himself for an idiot. It was an ill-conceived question. Ill-timed as well. All it had done was remind her of the true purpose of their being together this morning. And it wasn't for them to return the donkey to its rightful owners. It was for them to become better acquainted, with a view toward matrimony.

He may as well have asked her how many pets she planned to keep when they were married. It was outrageously presumptuous.

"Forgive me," he said. "I didn't mean to make you uncomfortable. I thought only to talk with you about what you love best."

She cautiously returned his gaze. "That was very kind of you."

"It was strategic. I didn't want to make any mistakes this time. Yet, that's exactly what I've done, haven't I?" He gave a humorless huff. "It seems I can't be in your company above five minutes without frightening you away."

Her mouth tilted in a faint smile. "You haven't frightened me."

James gave her a doubtful look. "No?"

"I find conversation difficult with strangers," she said. "But I'm not *scared* of them."

"Perhaps that's the trouble."

Her brows lifted. "That I'm not scared of you?"

"That we're still strangers," he said.

"Oh." Her cheeks colored. "I wouldn't say we were. Not exactly."

"But we're not friends, either."

She gripped the edge of the padded seat as the curricle bounced over an uneven patch of road. "Do you want to be my friend?"

"Very much so," he said.

The horses' hooves clip-clopped over the hard-packed earth of the road. The donkey's hoofbeats sounded behind, lighter and quicker.

Hannah cast a fleeting look back at the little creature before returning her attention to James. "You're well on your way. I can think of no one more deserving of friendship than a gentleman who would help an animal in need."

"I suppose that's a start," he said dryly.

"It is," she assured him. "I myself have never turned away an animal in need of rescuing. And..." She hesitated, suddenly shy again. "I don't imagine I ever would, not even when I marry."

James eyes briefly met hers. He felt the same surge of hope he'd felt yesterday when she'd confessed that she was glad he had returned to Bath. "Nor why should you."

"You wouldn't object to having a...a..."

"A menagerie?" He smiled slightly. "No." He guided the horses down the Lower Bristol Road. "My family's seat in

Hertfordshire is sizeable. There's ample room for animals, and plenty of staff to help care for them."

"You surely wouldn't wish to see it overrun."

"Worth House has witnessed countless family scandals over the centuries. If my sole contribution to the cannon is a pack of crossbreed dogs, I shall count myself fortunate indeed."

"Your sister has shared something of those scandals with me."

James cut her a piercing glance. "Has she?"

"About your grandfather having been a highwayman."

He suppressed a wince. Leave it to Kate to bandy about the worst of the Beresfords' history. Then again, she *was* marrying into the Heywood family. And it wasn't as if James's grandfather's infamy was a secret.

"Gentleman Jim, they called him," he said flatly.

Hannah's eyes lit. "Really?"

"Upon my honor."

"But how exciting it sounds! Just like a Penny Dreadful."

James gripped the reins hard. Highwaymen were frequently featured in the cheap, penny fiction of the day. Rather than villains, they were often portrayed as heroic figures. It was the furthest thing from the truth.

"Hardly that," he said. "My grandfather was a scoundrel who left my father in very bleak circumstances. There was nothing exciting about it."

Her smile dimmed. She was quiet a moment. "Were you named after him?"

"I was," he acknowledged grimly. "My great-grandfather and my parents had hoped I might restore dignity to the name."

"I'm confident you have."

"I've certainly given it my best effort." He turned the subject. "What about your name? Did you inherit it from a disreputable ancestor?"

"No, indeed. But my parents did like it very much. My father says it's straightforward, just as I am. The same, backwards and forwards. What you see is precisely what you get."

"I like what I see," James said, looking at her.

Hannah's cheeks turned petal pink, just as he'd hoped they would. She bent her head, briefly shielding her face from his view behind the brim of her straw bonnet. "I don't know how to reply when you say such things."

"Would you rather I didn't say them?"

"No, but...I should like to better prepare myself."

"Next time I compliment you," he said solemnly, "I'll take care to give you adequate warning."

She peeped at him from beneath her bonnet brim. "Now you're being absurd."

He returned his gaze to the road. "I've never been accused of that before."

"I don't expect you have. But I stand by my assessment." She folded her hands neatly in her lap. Her gloves were dyed to match her pelisse. "We were speaking of family scandals."

"Of which mine has many and yours has none."

"That isn't at all true."

"No?"

"My parents' elopement was a scandal."

James recalled hearing something of the old gossip about Hannah's parents when Charles and Kate had been courting. It was said that Captain Heywood had met his wife in London—a young beauty who, at the time, was rumored to have been betrothed to a duke. Some antiquated busybodies still maintained that the captain had kidnapped her and spirited her away to the country to be his unwilling bride.

"A nine-day scandal, if that," he said. "Elopements aren't in the same class as blatant criminal activity, even if they do inspire the London tabbies to talk."

"Not only the elopement," Hannah replied. "My father is a fearsome shot."

His mouth quirked at the seeming non sequitur. "Captain Heywood's reputation with a pistol is much admired. I wouldn't call it scandalous."

"Some might." She dropped her voice to a confidential whisper. "He once killed a gentleman who was threatening my mother."

James flashed her a sharp look as he guided the horses around a curve in the road. This was news to him. "When is this supposed to have happened?"

"It was years before I was born," she said. "Our housekeeper, Sara, confided it to me. She was my mother's lady's maid at the time. She said that my father put a bullet in the man's brain. And that my mother's wolfhound, Basil, bit the man for good measure."

James's brows lowered in a repressive frown. "Your housekeeper was very wrong to have mentioned it to you."

"Why?"

"Because it isn't a proper thing for a young lady to be hearing."

One wasn't meant to discuss shooting people around a female of any age, let alone sheltered young ladies in their first season.

"I thought it rather romantic," Hannah said.

"*Romantic?*"

"My father acted to protect my mother." She brushed one of her fluttering bonnet ribbons back from her cheek. "She was counted a rare beauty in her day, with many admirers from London who wanted to take her away and set her up as a trophy in their great houses. She refused them all to marry Papa. They love each other desperately."

"A moving story."

"It isn't a story. It's the truth. And it *is* scandalous, despite being romantic. It's one of the reasons my parents didn't host a come-out ball for me themselves, and why they thought it better for me to debut in Bath instead of in London. They didn't wish to risk my first season being sullied."

James gazed stonily at the road ahead, his hands steady as he reflexively guided the horses over the rise. He hadn't known the Heywoods' long-ago actions were still exacting a price from them. "I thought it was you who wanted to debut in Bath?"

"I did. But my preferences weren't the only factor. My parents are always a consideration. I'd no more cause pain to them than they would to me."

James's frown deepened. He'd been so consumed with rehabilitating the Beresfords' scandalous history, it hadn't occurred to him that Hannah's family might have their own scandal to deal with. If it was indeed true that they'd made a calculated decision to keep their daughter away from London...

But he had no good reason to doubt it.

Every interaction he'd had with Captain Heywood and his wife stood as proof of how much they loved their daughter. They were clearly too protective of her to subject her to even a whisper of unfavorable talk, even if that meant encouraging her to spend her first season in Bath.

James's own parents had been less obliging when it came to Kate. The Beresford way was more of the sword than of the shield. His sister had debuted in London without fear or apology, daring the society busybodies to say the worst.

And many of them had.

It hadn't been the first time the Beresfords had kicked a hornet's nest. One would think they enjoyed rekindling all the old gossip. That they relished the whispers about a stolen title. About James's father being a usurper—a cuckoo in the nest.

"I daresay it's why we have lived such a quiet life in Somerset," Hannah said. Her dark brows notched in an elegant line. "Charles didn't like it above half. He soon grew restless and desired to go to sea. But I love the solitude. I find it suits me very well."

"Perhaps because you don't know any different," James suggested.

Her gaze returned to his, vaguely affronted. "One needn't experience everything in the world to know where one's heart lies."

His attention lingered on her face. Despite everything she'd revealed to him, the revelations about her family's scandals, and the obstacles she would face if she ever removed to London. Yes, despite even that, his blood stirred with warmth. He had never met someone so confident in their own best instincts. "Your heart is your lodestar, is it?"

"In all things," she said. "Isn't yours?"

"Not generally. I find my head to be a more reliable compass."

"A person must use their powers of reason, naturally, but the right thing isn't always the most reasonable, I find."

James thought of his attraction to her. It surely wasn't reasonable. That was the precise reason he'd resisted it for so long. And yet...

Here he was.

"Perhaps not," he allowed.

Chapter Thirteen

Fallkirk's Farm lay just outside of the small village of Bidbury, at the edge of a beautiful green valley. A sign at the entrance to the drive proclaimed its name.

Hannah twisted in her seat in the curricle, glancing back at the donkey to see if he recognized his home. There appeared to be no change in the little creature's mood. He bore the same expression of alertness he'd worn when they had departed Camden Place.

"I thought he would be overjoyed," she said.

"It's been six months," James replied. "Perhaps he's forgotten?"

Hannah was skeptical. In her experience, animals didn't forget the homes they'd had or the treatment they'd received there, neither the good, *nor* the bad. She settled back in her seat as the curricle continued toward the farmhouse, rolling steadily over the hardpacked earth.

James was indeed an excellent driver, just as she had

assured her mother. Hannah had experienced little discomfort during their journey.

Not of the physical kind, anyway.

Good gracious, what had she been thinking to confide so much in him about her parents' history?

But she knew what she'd been thinking. She'd been attempting to reassure him about his own family's scandals. To show him that he wasn't alone.

And not only that.

She supposed she'd been not-so-subtly attempting to warn him. He already found so much objectionable in her person—her shyness, her seeming lack of confidence, her unwillingness to enter London society. But there were other obstacles too. Greater obstacles. Far better he should learn about them now.

If any of it had changed James's mind about pursuing her, Hannah couldn't tell. He was as civil to her as he'd been when they had set out. It was only when he looked at her that she could sense his conflict. He did indeed appear as though he was trying to solve a puzzle, just as Charles had said.

Unhappy thought.

She stared out at the lush fields of the farm, refocusing her attention on the task at hand. "It seems a pleasant place," she said. "Sweet William must have been quite content here before he was stolen away. I pray he will be so again."

"It will certainly be an improvement over pulling a cart," James replied.

"Indeed. I suspect the costermonger was unduly harsh with him. The way the poor creature cringed. It seems that..." She trailed off, her attention arrested by a startling sight in one of the paddocks that lined the long drive. It was an undersized donkey, serenely grazing on the grass. The little beast had one white ear.

Spying the distinctive feature, Hannah sat bolt upright in her seat. She stared at the donkey in alarm. "Oh no," she breathed. "Look, James."

James followed her gaze. His brows shot up. "Is *that* Sweet William?"

"I fear it is."

"Then the donkey we've brought back—"

"Is not," she said hollowly. "He must be a lookalike."

Up ahead, a portly man in a tweed cap stood at the gate of the cow pasture talking to two humbly dressed fellows. The farmer himself, Hannah presumed. He had a look of authority about him.

James pulled the curricle alongside him. "Do I have the privilege of addressing Mr. Fallkirk?"

"I'm Fallkirk," the farmer replied, coming over to meet them. "And who might you be, sir?"

"James Beresford, Viscount St. Clare," James said. "And this is Miss Heywood."

Hannah inclined her head to the man. She didn't speak. She was too embarrassed to do so. The donkey they'd brought with them was obviously *not* Sweet William. Not unless Sweet William had a near and identical relation.

Mr. Fallkirk bobbed his head at them both in greeting. Unlike the costermonger, he didn't appear unduly impressed by James's title. "How can I be of service yer lordship?"

"Miss Heywood and I had thought to return your missing donkey," James said.

Mr. Fallkirk exchanged a surprised look with his farmhands. Together, they walked behind the curricle to view the donkey in question. They returned almost immediately, a look of collective consternation on their faces.

"He do resemble m' daughter's donkey, I grant you," Mr. Fallkirk said. "But he's a mite too big. Sweet William is far smaller, as you see. He was returned to us a week ago. T'weren't stolen at all, as it transpired. He'd wandered off into the hills. One of my tenants found him and brought him back. M'daughter was delighted."

Hannah at last found her voice. "I'm very glad to hear it," she said. "Er, I don't suppose Miss Fallkirk would be interested in a second donkey?"

"Don't suppose she would, miss," Mr. Fallkirk said. "Sweet William is a territorial little rascal, prone to chasing off any other creature that invades his paddock. M' daughter spoiled him, that's the trouble. Thinks he's a dog not a farm animal."

"Yes, I see," Hannah said.

"You might offer this donkey at the sales this summer," Mr. Fallkirk suggested. "He's a good size for pulling one o' them fruit carts you see about town."

She winced.

"We shall consider it," James said. With that, he took his leave of the farmer, and turning the horses, exited the drive. He didn't say anything for a long while. Indeed, his countenance was uncommonly rigid.

Hannah steadfastly avoided his gaze. Good lord. What must he be thinking of her? Doubtless he was irritated or possibly even angry. She privately wondered if she owed him an apology for putting him to so much trouble.

But really, how was she to know it wasn't the right donkey?

"I am mortified," she declared at last. "Not only have I inconvenienced you, but to think, I accused that innocent costermonger of theft on a public street! I must find him and make my apologies."

"You don't owe him an apology."

"Indeed, I do."

"You didn't accuse him of theft outright, did you?"

"No, but I did greatly annoy him."

"For which he was handsomely compensated."

"Yes, he was, but—"

"Unless you mean to restore the donkey to him?"

"I most certainly don't," she said, appalled at the suggestion. "This donkey can't go back to a life of service. Not now he knows what a warm mash is and not after he's experienced a night in a comfortable stable. He deserves to be someone's pet, just like Sweet William is."

"*Your* pet?" James asked.

Hannah frowned. "As to that...I shall have to ask my parents." She considered the various complications. "Even if they said I could have him, the fact remains that we shall be in Bath for some time. It isn't a city well-disposed for keeping horses or donkeys. I should think it far better if he could return to the country with someone. Or perhaps be sent back with someone's groom who would look after him in the manner to which he's become accustomed."

"Someone," he repeated. "Anyone in particular?"

She gave him a hopeful look. "You wouldn't have need of a donkey, would you?"

James burst out laughing.

Hannah started. She'd never seen him laugh before. The

action wrought a dramatic change in his countenance. The hard lines of his face softened, the corners of his eyes crinkled, and he smiled—such a smile! It was dazzling and warm, making him at once more handsome and more human.

Her own mouth quivered in reflexive response. Soon, she was laughing too. "Oh, what a muddle. But you must own I haven't been completely out of order. This donkey *does* bear a remarkable resemblance to Sweet William."

"Quite remarkable. He will make someone a handsome pet, I'm sure." James paused, adding wryly, "That someone being me."

Hannah's bosom swelled with gratitude. She beamed up at him. "Oh, thank you, James! You won't be sorry, I promise you."

He held her gaze for a moment. "How can I be sorry when I've made you smile?"

"I often do smile."

"Not like that," he said. "Not at me."

Her expression was dimmed by a trace of self-consciousness. "Haven't I?"

"Never." He turned the horses back onto the Bath Road. "When you came to stay at Beasley Park, I often saw you laughing and smiling with my brothers. I confess, I was envious of them."

Hannah was certain he was being gallant. Her heart nevertheless skipped a beat.

To think that he'd been observing her even then! That he'd coveted her smiles! It was excessively romantic.

"Yes," she said, "but Ivo and Jack laughed and smiled too. You never did. Indeed, I'd never heard you laugh at all until five minutes ago."

This seemed to surprise him. "What? Never?"

She shook her head.

"I'm not incapable of it," he said.

"Only very rarely amused?"

A frown clouded his brow. "I suppose, when one is the heir, one learns to maintain a certain dignity."

"Laughter is undignified?"

"Not laughter. A lack of control."

It was very much as Hannah had suspected. "Have you always been so adept at keeping your countenance?" she asked. "Were you never..."

"What?"

"Less strategic?"

His eyes found hers as he drove. "It's difficult to dispense with strategy when I want something as much as I want you."

Hannah's heart performed another disconcerting somersault. She was keenly conscious of the scorching heat rising in her cheeks, but this time she didn't shyly lower her eyes. She returned his gaze steadily. "You don't need to be strategic with me," she said. "I only ask that you be yourself."

Chapter Fourteen

James drove Hannah back to Camden Place in a far more optimistic frame of mind than he'd been in when he'd arrived to collect her. They had experienced something together this morning. Smiles. Laughter. A shared sense of the absurd. It had lent a lightness to their conversation that had never been present before. She had been, for a short time, suddenly and remarkably at ease with him.

She had also asked him to be himself.

James wasn't entirely confident he could oblige her.

He had spent so much of his life keeping ruthless control of his emotions that he'd forgotten what it was like to relax his hold. To be impulsive. Frivolous. Fun. The very qualities that characterized his reckless younger siblings.

Unlike them, James had had no older brother to pave the way, either at school or in fashionable society. He'd been the one to take all the slings and arrows. To deal with the slurs, the slander, the outright insults. There had been only one way of doing so. Rather than rising to the bait, engaging in endless bouts of fisticuffs over his family's honor, he'd learned to affect an air of intimidatingly cold reserve.

At the time, it had been a studied copy of his father at his most formidable moments. But James no longer had to affect that glacial formidability, to don it like a suit of armor as he'd done during his years at Eton and Oxford. It had become who he was, as natural to him as breathing.

The closest he'd come to abandoning his control was in his decision to pursue Hannah Heywood. She wasn't part of his master plan for the Beresford family. She didn't *fit*. And in the end, it hadn't mattered. His attraction to her had overshadowed all sensible concern. Just like that, he'd been willing to cast away years of planning and calculation. Tempted to give it all up if only he could have her for his own.

James despised the weakness in himself, even as he relished every moment spent in Hannah's company.

On returning, he escorted her into the house. He was on the verge of inquiring when he might see her again, when a footman approached them.

"Captain Heywood awaits you in the library, my lord," the footman said.

Hannah's hands stilled in the act of untying her pink satin bonnet ribbons. A glimmer of anxiety shone in her eyes. "I'd forgotten he wished to speak with you."

"I hadn't," James replied. "If you will excuse me?"

"Of course," she said.

He bowed to her before following the footman from the hall. The library was at the back of the residence in a similar location to the library in the Beresfords' house on the Circus.

Captain Heywood was inside, seated behind a carved walnut desk in the corner. He appeared to be writing a letter. He didn't rise. "Lord St. Clare," he said. "Please, sit down."

James took a seat in one of the leather-upholstered chairs across from him. The desk between them gave the meeting an air of formality. No doubt Captain Heywood had intended it to. James was, after all, a suitor for his daughter's hand. A once-spurned suitor who had had the temerity to return to the scene of his defeat. And Captain Heywood was nothing if not a protective father.

A *very* protective father.

Indeed, if Hannah's story was to be believed, Captain Heywood was cold-bloodedly ruthless when it came to the defense of his family.

James hadn't seen it in him initially. But he could see it now quite clearly, even as the captain finished his letter. The steely glint in his eyes, the sternness of his brow, and the steadiness of his hand as he held his quill pen. The same steadiness with which he was reputed to hold a pistol.

Yet Hannah had claimed her father was a romantic too. *That* James couldn't see. Whatever softness Captain Heywood's granite-hard demeanor was shielding was reserved for his family alone.

At length, the captain set down his quill. He tucked his unfinished letter under the blotter. "I trust everything has been resolved with the stolen donkey?"

"It has, sir," James replied. "After a fashion. It seems the donkey now belongs to me." He gave the captain a brief summary of what had happened at Fallkirk's Farm.

The story provoked a rare flash of humor in Captain Heywood's otherwise flinty expression. "I can't say I'm surprised," he said. "There have been many occasions over the years when championing an animal on behalf of my wife or my daughter has had the same result."

James's mouth hitched briefly at one corner. "Do you mean to say that you've found yourself the unwitting owner of an animal or two?"

"Or ten," Captain Heywood said. "A man soon grows accustomed."

James could easily imagine himself in the same predicament. The prospect wasn't an unpleasant one. Not if Hannah was part of the picture. "I count it a small price to pay for the privilege of knowing your daughter," he said.

"It heartens me to hear you say so," the captain replied solemnly, "considering the fact that she rejected you. And in no uncertain terms, I believe."

James's expression sobered. "Yes, she did," he acknowledged. "I suspect you knew she would."

Captain Heywood didn't deny it. "My daughter was raised to know her worth. I knew she was not likely to settle for less than a love match."

James flinched. "I'm well aware she isn't in love with me."

"Yet, here you are." Captain Heywood sat back in his chair. He surveyed James's face with a thoughtful frown. "*Why* are you here?"

James saw no point in wasting either of their time with long-winded explanations. Not when his reasons for returning to Bath could be distilled into five simple words. "I gave up too soon."

"Some would say you gave up at exactly the right moment. A man who has had his proposals refused has good reason to quit the field."

James recalled those bleak, regret-filled weeks in London. He'd spent every day of them raking himself over the coals, first for having proposed to Hannah at all, and then for having done so without having first made an effort to win her heart.

"Which I did," he said. "Until I came to my senses."

Captain Heywood regarded him in silence for a long moment. "I presume you're aware of the effect of your returning?"

"In relation to Miss Heywood?"

"In relation to the whole of Bath society. Your presence here looms large. If you mean to make yourself a fixture at every entertainment to which my daughter is invited, you will soon drive away all competition for her hand."

Good, James thought uncharitably. But he didn't show it. And he certainly didn't say it.

"I'm not concerned about competition," he replied instead. "It's Miss Heywood I'm interested in, nothing else. I hope that, with time and effort, I might prove to her that she could one day find happiness with me."

"An admirable answer," Captain Heywood said.

"It's the truth, sir. I was in error before, approaching her too hastily. It's not a mistake I intend to repeat. I mean to do things properly this time."

"Also, admirable."

James felt a flicker of unease. Hannah's father was an incredibly difficult man to read. It was impossible to predict whether he would endorse James renewing his suit or put an end to it here and now. James very much feared it would be the latter.

"Do you disapprove?" he asked abruptly.

"I neither approve nor disapprove," Captain Heywood

said. "My only purpose in summoning you here was to issue a warning."

James tensed.

"Your family and mine are soon to be connected by marriage," Captain Heywood said. "That allows for a certain informality between us. But know this. Regardless of any respect I might hold for your parents, if you cause my daughter even a moment of pain, you shall answer to me."

James didn't take the warning lightly. "Understood."

"That's not all." Captain Heywood's face grew more serious still. "I want something from you, lad."

"Anything, sir," James said promptly.

"At the first indication that my daughter doesn't return your interest, I want your word as a gentleman that you will leave Bath."

James's stomach sank. Hell's teeth. He had walked neatly into that trap, hadn't he?

"I won't permit you to stand in the way of her finding true happiness, whether that happiness lies with another gentleman or back home with her mother and me. With you out of the way, she will be free to decide what's best for her."

"I would never stand in the way of her happiness," James said.

Captain Heywood was unmoved. "I want your word."

James saw no way to avoid giving it. He stiffly inclined his head in grudging acceptance of the captain's terms. "Very well," he answered. "You have it."

Chapter Fifteen

Hannah arranged her skirts around her as she knelt down on the striped blanket Lady Carleton had spread over the grass. It was one of many such blankets scattered about the tree-studded park, each of them occupied by fashionable ladies and gentlemen, talking and laughing, and dining on the offerings from their picnic hampers. Liveried servants stood about them, pouring glasses of champagne and preparing plates of cold chicken, ham, and tongue.

"We are fortunate in the weather," Lady Carleton said as she unfurled her parasol.

"Indeed, we are," Hannah agreed. The sky was clear and the sun was shining, with only a whisper of a breeze drifting over the hills to alleviate the warmth of the early afternoon.

"When one has hosted as many picnic parties as I have over the decades, one learns how easily such gatherings can go awry. A single rain shower and the whole affair must be removed indoors. Either that or cancelled altogether."

"This is my first picnic party," Hannah admitted. She'd

donned a new white muslin dress with a primrose satin ribbon sash for the occasion, and had worn her prettiest straw bonnet. It was in the way of being her armor. She had suspected she would need it.

Charles was meeting with his solicitor this afternoon and had been unable to accompany her. Instead, Hannah had traveled to the picnic site in the Carletons' barouche, every minute of the journey wishing she could plead a headache or a fever—anything to be permitted to return home.

It was poor spirited of her, she knew. But there was something dreadfully intimidating about a picnic. There was no structure to it. No formality. Unlike a ball, where everything proceeded in accordance with the program of dances, or a dinner, where there existed a seating arrangement. At a picnic party, people moved freely from blanket to blanket. They clustered in self-selected groups, giggling and whispering. Some even wandered off together, to go exploring or to engage in games or sport.

From the moment they'd arrived, Hannah had felt herself on the outside of things. It was why she'd resolved to cleave to her hostess. She'd had little choice in Charles's absence. As for James, she wasn't entirely certain he'd been invited, let alone whether he'd be in attendance.

Lady Carleton smiled at her. "Then we must make sure you are well entertained." She tipped her parasol, shielding her face from the sun. "You must join the young people. There is Miss Fieldstone. And I see Miss Paley with Lord Fennick. She has just arrived from London yesterday. A charming girl, from an estimable family. Her father has come to take the waters. He suffers dreadfully from his gout."

Hannah had met Miss Fieldstone at a dinner party, and had danced with Lord Fennick for a single set at her first ball. However, she had not yet met Miss Paley. She was a dainty, porcelain-skinned blond, with a decided air about her. Mr. Fennick and another gentleman were dancing attendance on her, giving every indication that they considered Miss Paley to be the belle of the picnic.

"Oh no," Hannah swiftly objected. "I'm quite happy to remain here with you."

"You are exceedingly polite, my dear, but I know better. Miss Paley!" Lady Carleton called out to the young lady. "Allow me to introduce you to Miss Heywood."

Miss Paley gave their hostess a tight smile. She murmured something to her companion before rising from her blanket, with his assistance, and coming to join them. She wore a dress of apple green muslin, with satin trimmed skirts that floated around her like a bell. "Lady Carleton. Miss Heywood. A pleasure."

"I have just been attempting to persuade Miss Heywood to abandon my poor self for more enlivening company," Lady Carleton said. "Do be a dear and take her with you. This is her first season, and I am resolved that she make the most of it."

"If you wish it, ma'am." Miss Paley's dark eyes settled on Hannah. Her expression was cool. "Miss Heywood?"

Hannah stood, smoothing her skirts. She had told James that she wasn't afraid of strangers. That much had been true. But her shyness often manifested as something very like fear. It made her palms grow clammy and her stomach tremble. She did her best to ignore it. "Thank you," she said. "I'm obliged to you."

"Not at all." As they approached Miss Paley's blanket,

Lord Fennick moved toward them. Miss Paley repelled him with a wave of her hand. "Shall we walk?" she asked Hannah.

"If you like."

"I would like it," Miss Paley said. "What I *don't* like is popping up and down from the grass like a jack-in-the-box. It is most inconvenient."

Lord Fennick trailed doggedly after them. "Your parasol, Miss Paley."

Miss Paley accepted it from him. "Fennick? I believe you know Miss Heywood?"

"Miss Heywood." Lord Fennick offered a perfunctory bow.

"Sir," Hannah replied, inclining her head.

"Come," Miss Paley said to Hannah. "Let us take a turn about the park." She strode away, leaving Lord Fennick behind them.

Hannah kept pace with Miss Paley, walking with her across the grass and toward the tree-lined dirt path that wended its way around the grounds.

"I'm not familiar with the name Heywood," Miss Paley said. "You are not, I presume, from London?"

"I am not. My parents reside but fifty miles from here, near the village of Heycombe."

"Your father is a squire?"

"A retired captain of the army. He is the second son of the Earl of Gordon."

Miss Paley's eyes flashed to Hannah with sharpened attention. She looked her up and down. "And you are having your season in *Bath?* Whatever for?"

"I prefer it," Hannah answered simply.

"The society is not very refined here."

"I have not found it lacking."

"You must take my word for it. I had my first season in London. The quality of parties there is far superior to anything you could find in Bath, or Brighton, or Tunbridge Wells. Had my father not needed to take the waters for his health, I would be in London still. I can't imagine why anyone would ever wish to have their season anywhere else." Miss Paley gave a disdainful sniff. "But, I suppose, if you desire to wed a farmer or a man of business, Bath is as good a place as any to find such a person."

Hannah's mouth curved in spite of herself. She had met many self-important people during her first weeks in Bath, but surely Miss Paley was the most self-important of them all. "I confess, I had not considered my future husband's profession."

"I prefer a husband with no profession," Miss Paley returned. "That is to say, a gentleman." She opened her parasol. The miniscule white lace shade was so tiny as to be of no practical use at all. "Lady Carleton informs me that Viscount St. Clare is presently in Bath."

Hannah glanced at Miss Paley in surprise. "Do you know his lordship?"

"I should say so. I saw him but a few days ago in London. We waltzed together at a ball hosted by the Marquess of Deane. St. Clare is an excellent partner."

A knot of mingled disbelief and astonishment formed in Hannah's breast. She had not considered that James might have attended balls while he was in London. And she hadn't imagined him waltzing with other ladies. Not when he'd professed to be thinking of her.

A fork appeared in the road ahead. The right turning

led over the hill. The left, back to the expanse of lawn where the rest of the picnic party remained.

Miss Paley guided Hannah to the left. "The marquess's daughter, Lady Augusta, is a particular friend of mine. Perhaps you've met?"

"We have not," Hannah said.

"Pity. She is a most superior person. I have heard that she and St. Clare might one day—" Miss Paley broke off, coming to an abrupt halt. She stared out at the lawn. "Upon my soul. There is the very man."

Hannah stilled. She followed Miss Paley's gaze. Her heart stopped. It was James, sure enough, looking dashing in fashionable morning dress, the sun gleaming in his golden hair. He came to join them on the path.

Miss Paley's face spread into a dazzling smile. "Lord St. Clare. We meet again."

James bowed. "Miss Paley." His gray eyes met Hannah's. "Miss Heywood."

"My lord," Hannah murmured.

Miss Paley looked between them, her smile gone flat. "You are acquainted?"

"Lord St. Clare's sister is betrothed to my older brother," Hannah said.

"Oh?" Miss Paley's tone took on a note of censure. "You might have mentioned such happy news when we met in London, my lord."

"It quite slipped my mind," James said, still looking at Hannah.

"Please pass on my congratulations to Lady Katherine," Miss Paley said.

"I will convey them to her at the first opportunity," he said. "Miss Heywood? The ruins of a Norman church lie not far over that hill. I had planned to explore them further, if you would care to join me?"

Miss Paley's lips thinned. "That dreary place? It's nearly a mile away."

"An easy enough walk," James said. "If Miss Heywood is at all interested."

Hannah managed a small smile. "I would very much like to see the ruins," she said. "Thank you, my lord."

JAMES OFFERED HIS ARM TO HANNAH AS THEY ascended the hill, and she took it. "Lady Carleton assured me you would be here today," he said.

"You spoke to her?"

"I called on her yesterday evening to pay my respects. One can't arrive in Bath without notifying its leading hostess. Not if one has any hopes of attending the best parties."

Hannah didn't reply. They walked together in silence for several steps. "How do you know Miss Paley?" she asked at last.

Ah.

So that was it.

James had sensed there was something amiss. The smile she'd given him when he'd arrived had been guarded. Even the hand she'd rested on his arm was light and noncommittal, as though she might remove it any moment and draw away from him again. He felt a flicker of apprehension.

And of satisfaction too, he was ashamed to admit.

If Hannah was in any ways jealous of Miss Paley, it could only mean that she was coming to care for him a little.

"She's the sister of a fellow I knew at Eton," he said. "I met her many years ago when I went to stay with him over a summer holiday. It isn't a visit I look back on with any degree of fondness."

"She told me that she saw you in London but a few days ago, and that she danced with you at a ball given by the Marquess of Deane. Is that true?"

"It is."

"Is that what you did while you were in London? Attended balls?"

"Among other things."

Hannah fell quiet again. She remained silent until they had nearly crested the hill. "I had not thought—" She broke off before she could finish.

James slowed on the path to look at her. "What hadn't you thought?"

"That you were in such good spirits while you were away."

"I wasn't."

"Miss Paley claims that, during your brief time in town, you resumed your courtship of the marquess's daughter, Lady Augusta."

James somehow managed to keep his countenance. Whatever his actions in London, and whatever his thoughts about the suitability of Lady Augusta as a prospective bride, he had never had the smallest intention of hurting Hannah.

"If that's what Miss Paley has told you, she has been woefully misinformed," he said.

"Then, you didn't resume your courtship?"

"There was no courtship to resume."

"And you didn't waltz with the lady?"

His brows sank. "I did, but... It was no more than a civility."

"I see." Hannah's hand fell from his arm.

James keenly felt the absence of it. "You're displeased with me."

"I haven't any right to be."

"You have more right than anyone." He caught her gently by the forearm, bringing her to a halt in front of him beneath the branches of an oak tree. "I was miserable in London."

She gazed up at him. Her eyes held an aching uncertainty.

In that moment, James would have done anything to assuage it. "I spent every moment at the boxing saloon or with my fencing master, attempting to rid myself of these feelings I have for you," he said. "And yes, I attended the marquess's ball. I stupidly thought that your rejection might make another lady more palatable to me. Obviously, it didn't. Even knowing that you didn't want to marry me, I couldn't fix my interest on anyone else."

Hannah's mouth trembled. "Your sister described Lady Augusta as a paragon."

"She is."

"And I am not, as my behavior yesterday will have amply proved to you."

"I have no expectations in that regard," he said. "I was a fool to have implied that I did." He offered her a slight smile. "As for your rescue of the donkey, you will hear no criticism from me. I thought you conducted yourself magnificently."

Hannah's chin dipped down with embarrassment. "I

don't know about magnificent. It was an awful blunder, even if it was ultimately for the good."

"As a man who has lately made several awful blunders, I can but commiserate."

It was her turn to smile. This time it wasn't a guarded one. It was warm, and a little rueful. "How is he?" she asked. "Have you made any arrangements for him yet?"

"At present, he's comfortably ensconced with my horses at the Bull and Crown. Tomorrow, however, one of my grooms will be escorting him to Beasley Park. There are few places in the world more idyllic for human or animal. I'm confident he'll be happy there. Or as happy as a donkey can be." He offered her his arm again. "Shall we continue to the church?"

She tucked her hand in the crook of his elbow. "Donkeys are capable of great happiness," she informed him. "Haven't you ever heard them braying with joy when they recognize a friend in the pasture? It is the most heart-warming sound."

"I shall take your word for it," James said.

Together they walked on over the rise and down the serpentine path along a small woodland. The church was visible in the distance, its crumbling stone edifice rising amidst a stand of trees. It had walls, but no roof. Only the tower remained intact.

"Have you been here before?" he asked.

"Never," she replied. "Have you?"

"Once, when I was a lad. My brothers and I explored the ruins while my parents lunched on the grass with Kate. She threw a dreadful tantrum when she couldn't come with us. Her face turned as red as a ripe tomato."

Hannah's lips quivered with reluctant amusement. "Poor thing. Why didn't you allow her to join you?"

"She was but a small child at the time. We none of us wanted the charge of her. Not very gallant, I know, but we were scarcely much older ourselves."

"Did you and your brothers play together often as children?"

"As often as any brothers might." James glanced at her. "Does that surprise you?"

"It does, a little, I confess. You never joined in with Ivo and Jack's merriment when I visited Beasley Park, or when your family came to stay at Heywood House."

"No," he acknowledged, his expression sobering. "Things changed after I went away to school." He paused. "*I* changed."

"How?"

"I grew up."

Her eyes briefly met his as they continued down the path. Her gaze was soft with understanding. "Was it at school that you learned to wield such control over your emotions?"

A frown creased his brow. "I don't know. Probably."

"I begin to think you had a difficult time there."

His mouth twisted in a fleeting, humorless smile. "Everyone has a difficult time at school. Young boys are savages. They grow into unpleasant men. One can either learn to ignore it or else spend his days in an endless succession of brawls over his family's honor."

"Is *that* what the trouble was? Your family?"

"In my case? Yes. For the most part. Paley and Fennick greatly enjoyed baiting me on the subject."

"Lord Fennick?" she repeated. "I wasn't aware you were at school with him."

"It didn't bear mentioning."

"He's here today. He was sitting with Miss Paley on her picnic blanket."

James looked at her. "So long as he wasn't sitting with you."

A soft flush crept up her throat. "Indeed not. I did dance with him once, but that was quite enough. Now I know he was unpleasant to you, I shall take pains to avoid him."

James was touched by her show of loyalty. It was yet another small proof that she was coming to care for him. He marked it well, adding it to the other evidence he'd been collecting. Taken altogether it surely had to weigh in his favor.

"Who were you sharing your picnic blanket with, then?" he asked her.

"Lady Carleton," she answered.

"Perhaps you will permit me to join you when we return?"

The blush at her throat suffused into her cheeks in a delicate, watercolor stain. "I would like that."

James's blood warmed. He felt at once both besotted by and profoundly protective of her. He covered her hand with his on his arm. "Have you eaten yet?"

"Not yet, no," she said. "I had not accounted for all the cold meats being brought. It's been difficult to find anything that hasn't mingled with them in the picnic hampers."

"I'll find something for you when we return," he promised her.

She gave him a grateful smile. "An orange would suffice."

"You shall have one," he vowed.

The church loomed ahead. James led Hannah into what remained of the churchyard. It was overrun with grass and thorny bushes and brambles. Crooked headstones peeped out from the overgrowth. The graves were hundreds of years old, the chiseled names of their occupants worn to near invisibility over the centuries.

Hannah let go of his arm in order to clutch her skirts. She raised them above her ankles as they picked their way through the graveyard. "It doesn't seem right for the church to be abandoned. Not when people are still buried here."

"The villagers could hardly hold services without a roof."

"They could repair it."

"They've no incentive to do so. There's a church in the next village that fits the purpose. I presume most of them attend services there."

She gazed up at the tower. "Can we go inside?"

"If you wish."

"Is it safe?"

"Safe enough." James offered his hand to her to assist her over the stones. She took it. "Mind your head. The ceiling is rather low."

"Normans weren't very tall, I gather."

He smiled. "Perhaps not." He led her through the entrance of the tower to the winding stair. The steps were solid stone. So too were the walls. They were in no danger, but the way was steep and narrow. It was impossible for two people to ascend except single-file.

Hannah climbed ahead of him, still holding his hand. "It's exceedingly cold up here."

"It was when I visited too," he said. "Jack claimed it was because the tower is haunted."

"Haunted?" She stopped short on the step above, turning abruptly to look at him.

James inelegantly bumped into her. Hannah's foot slipped on the stone. She fell against him, her hands clutching his shoulders for balance. He caught her waist, steadying her before they both lost their footing. "Careful," he said.

Their faces were nearly level. James found himself staring into her eyes. She looked back at him in breathless silence.

And he didn't think. He didn't strategize. For once, he acted purely with his heart, doing what he most wanted to do. What he'd dreamed of doing from almost the first moment of their acquaintance.

He bent his head and he kissed her.

Chapter Sixteen

Hannah's eyes fell closed as James's mouth captured hers. Her body listed against his. Indeed, she may well have sighed. She wasn't entirely certain. Her mind had gone to porridge. It was impossible to breathe, let alone think. She could only feel. The granite-hard breadth of his shoulders beneath her fingers. The unyielding strength of his arms encircling her waist. And his lips, warm and sweet, as he kissed her slowly, tenderly.

Her own lips softened under his. Their breath mingled. It was a shocking intimacy. And there was no mistaking the gentleman with whom she was sharing it. It was James Beresford. Not the icily controlled viscount who had intimidated her all those months ago at Beasley Park, but the *real* James. The man who had been miserable after she'd rejected his proposal. The one who had risked his heart and his pride to come back to her, knowing full well he might be rejected again.

It was surely that which made him hold her a little too tightly, kiss her with a trifle too much heat.

Hannah didn't mind it. Quite the reverse. Her heart thumped rapidly, and her blood surged in her veins. She curved a hand around his neck. "*James*," she murmured.

The single whispered word seemed to recall him to his senses.

His mouth stilled on hers. At length, he drew back. His color was high, his chest rising and falling with unusual rapidity. "I have been unforgivably forward," he said gruffly.

"Oh no," she objected, breathless. "You haven't— That is, it wasn't—"

"Forgive me. I did not bring you here to take advantage of you."

"You haven't taken advantage of me. Indeed, if you hadn't come to my aid, I'd likely have fallen down the steps."

"A generous depiction of what just occurred. I must beg your pardon."

She looked into his eyes. For all his sudden formality, he was still holding her fast in his arms. "Pray, don't spoil it," she said softly.

He stared down at her, his brows notched. "Hannah—"

"Miss Heywood?" a lady's voice drifted into the tower from the churchyard. "Lord St. Clare? We have come to join your explorations!"

Hannah swiftly withdrew her hands from James's shoulder in the same moment he abruptly released her from his arms. "Good heavens," she said under her breath. "It's Miss Paley."

"They must be here," a male voice replied from below. "There's nothing else of interest for miles."

"She isn't alone," James said to Hannah.

Hannah stepped back onto the step above. She hastily smoothed her dress in case the muslin had been unduly wrinkled during their embrace. When she'd finished, she gave James a terse nod.

He nodded once in reply before answering Miss Paley and her companion. "We're on the stairs!"

In short order, the sound of Miss Paley's skirts brushing against the stone announced her presence on the winding steps. She soon appeared behind James. "You are braver than I, to have ventured up so far," she said. "What if this pitiful structure should tumble down on all our heads?"

Lord Fennick came after her. An almost imperceptible flicker of annoyance crossed James's face at the sight of him. "It's stood for centuries," Lord Fennick said. "It's not going to fall today."

Hannah glanced behind him. "Is it only the two of you, sir?"

"Lord, no," he replied. "We've made a party of it."

"The others are in the churchyard," Miss Paley said as the four of them continued up the tower steps. "Miss Fieldstone has brought a hamper."

THE REMAINDER OF THE PICNIC PASSED IN A BLUR of activity. Miss Paley, Lord Fennick, and the others chattered, laughed, and made raucous sport with each other as they explored the ruins, dined in the churchyard, and duly walked back over the hill to rejoin the rest of the party.

Hannah endured it all with what she hoped wasn't too much shyness. She smiled when she was expected to and politely made her replies to questions, all the while privately possessed of a tumult of emotion.

If James was similarly afflicted, she couldn't tell. The moment the others had arrived, his face had reverted to its cooly unreadable mask. He was still civil. Still attentive. He'd brought her a plate of bread, cheese, and nuts, and had sat beside her on the picnic blanket, gallantly peeling her an orange, but there was no more privacy to be had with him. No chance for a quiet moment alone and no opportunity for intimate conversation.

Hannah supposed it was for the best. What could she possibly say to him after they'd shared a kiss like that?

It had been her first. That much must have been evident to him. She was grateful he hadn't remarked on it. It was bad enough that he'd apologized to her—and multiple times too.

A disconcerting end to an otherwise wonderful experience.

She was resolved not to be offended by it. No doubt most gentlemen who had kissed a respectable young lady would have behaved thus. To be sure, many of them would have followed their kiss with a proposal.

The possibility that James's thoughts might be trending in that direction, did nothing to calm Hannah's already frayed nerves.

She was growing closer to him, it was true, but she wasn't prepared to revisit her decision on spending the rest of her life with him. It was too soon. There was too much about their fragile future that was still uncertain.

At the end of the picnic, James handed her up into the Carletons' barouche himself. "Will you be attending the dance at Lord and Lady Teesdales' Friday evening?" he asked her.

"I will," she said. "Might I see you there?"

James's gaze held hers, unwavering. "You may depend on it."

JAMES WAS HALFWAY TO HIS WAITING CURRICLE when Fennick's voice sounded behind him.

"Didn't expect to see you back in Bath so soon after you left it," he drawled. "But then, your family estate is near here, is it not?"

James was in no mood for Fennick's needling. Not after he had just spent several hours privately fuming at having his limited time with Hannah interrupted by Miss Paley, Fennick, and the others. A party, they'd called it. Torture more like. All that affected laughter and inane conversation as they'd wandered the ruins and irreverently dined among the headstones.

The worst of it was that James suspected he should be grateful for the interruption. In the aftermath of kissing Hannah, his normally functional brain had been running on more instinct than sense. A gentlemanly instinct, to be sure. Given the chance, he'd like have proposed to Hannah again. And when she'd rejected him—as she was sure to have done—he would have been honor bound to leave Bath, just as he'd promised her father he would.

It was a damnable situation. And not at all like him, either. He didn't go about kissing young ladies indiscreetly. And he didn't lose control. Not like that. Not ever.

He continued to his curricle where Bill awaited him, holding the horses' heads.

"Beasley Park, wasn't it?" Fennick pressed, following after him. "Your mother's ancestral home as I remember."

"Do you have something you desire to say to me, Fennick?" James inquired as he came to a halt beside his team of matched grays.

Fennick stopped next to him. His mustache was drooping, his pale face slightly sunburned from lounging on the lawn without his hat. He'd spent many moments during luncheon observing James and Hannah with a malicious gleam in his eye. "Merely indulging my curiosity."

"Indulge it elsewhere," James said.

Fennick chuckled at James's tone of command. "You haven't changed a whit since school, have you? Every inch of you the same—too arrogant by half. The only oddity is why a man of your ambition has lowered himself to spending the season in Bath."

"You presume I owe you an explanation?" James turned to address Bill. "How are they?"

"Ready to go, my lord," Bill said. "I watered them and walked them not half an hour ago."

"Good lad," James said.

Fennick remained standing beside the curricle as James took the reins from his tiger. "Miss Heywood is a queer little creature," he said.

James outwardly stilled, even as a frightening surge of rage ignited in his veins. It took the whole of his faculties to master it. Once he did, he handed the driving reins back to his tiger, and slowly turned to face Lord Fennick.

The blackguard's lip curled with satisfaction at having successfully hit his mark. "Not anything special, I thought," he continued unrepentantly. "But your interest encourages me to give her a second look."

"Is this what you've been reduced to since Oxford?" James asked in a voice of perilous calm. "Threatening respectable young ladies?"

"I'm a man of property, with a title to my name, and an unsullied bloodline to match—unlike some other gentlemen I could mention. The suggestion of paying my addresses to Miss Heywood can hardly be construed as a threat." Fennick smirked. "She colors up prettily, doesn't she? One might almost be willing to overlook her peculiarities."

"Stay away from her," James said.

"And there are several. Miss Heywood appears to—"

"Don't even speak her name."

Fennick broke off. "Why not? She's just the diversion I need to amuse me this season. More amusing still, now I've discovered she's your little pet. I predict I'll be speaking her name frequently."

"You won't," James assured him.

"Or what?"

"Or your unsullied bloodline will end with you."

Fennick's satisfied smile froze on his face. His eyes narrowed. "Now *that* sounds like a threat."

Bill's gaze darted between the two men as he listened with rapt attention. He would doubtless be providing a detailed report of the entire exchange in the servants' quarters this evening.

"It's not an idle one," James said.

Fennick uttered a snort of disbelief. "You're bluffing."

James took a menacing step toward him. He had ignored countless remarks from Fennick and his kind over the years. Snide comments about James's grandfather having been a highwayman, about the legitimacy of James's father's birth, and about James's own questionable claim to the earldom. Never once had James succumbed to the impulse for violence, despite the urge for it being baked into his bones.

But this was different.

This was Hannah.

She wasn't like Ivo, Jack, or even Kate, who could brush off vile gossip and mean-spirited whispers as effortlessly as if they were swatting away a troublesome gnat. Hannah was gentle. Sensitive. Exceedingly precious to him.

James wouldn't permit anyone to threaten her, even if it meant dispatching the threatener himself.

He loomed over Fennick. "Try me," he said softly, "and find out."

Chapter Seventeen

"Your note said it was urgent," Hannah said. She sat across from Mattie in the vicarage's small parlor. Her maid, Ernsby, was disposed near the window, having accompanied Hannah to Locksmore in the Heywoods' carriage.

It was the first time Hannah had been invited to the Winthrops' modest home. Located but a few miles from Camden Place, it was a thatch-roofed structure, with a neatly arranged interior, furnished in dark wood and overstuffed chintz. Two aging wolfhounds were stretched out at odd angles on the worn carpet, and a well-fed black cat was curled up in a wingchair.

A grandmotherly-looking housekeeper had brought in the tea tray the moment Hannah had arrived.

Mattie was unusually somber as she lifted the white porcelain pot to pour out their tea. "It *is* urgent." She passed Hannah a cup. "Though not, perhaps, as dire as I made it seem."

"Is it about my cat article?" Hannah had posted the

piece to Mattie several days ago and had yet to hear back from her.

"No, no. That is...it does concern your essay, but not for any reason you might think."

"Then you approved of it?"

"Without question. Your writing is succinct and non-judgmental, with a good helping of sentiment."

Hannah winced. "Was I *too* sentimental?"

"Not at all. Sentiment is a good thing for the cause. Often, the best way to reach a person's mind is through their heart." Mattie took a fortifying sip of her tea. "No. It's not anything you've done, but something *I* have done, quite unintentionally."

"You had better just have out with it," Hannah said. "It cannot be that bad."

Mattie lowered her cup back to its saucer, her brow furrowed in a deep line. "I was, perhaps, overambitious when I said that the *Animal Advocate* would be a monthly publication. I have been beside myself this past week assembling all the elements together for the printer. I might have predicted that something would go wrong."

Hannah waited.

"The crux of it is..." Mattie moistened her lips. "I forgot to use only your initial on the attribution for your article. It has gone to print with your full name, Hannah Heywood."

"Oh." Hannah blinked. "That isn't too—"

"It's bad," Mattie said.

"Surely not. My contributions have already been published once with my name."

"The horse article was published with your initial. The H might have stood for Henry, or Harry, or Hal. Now, however, everyone will know that the article was penned by a Hannah."

Hannah felt a stirring of pride at the prospect. "I am glad for them to know," she said. "The sentiments I expressed in that article are nothing I'm ashamed of."

"I agree. You've done nothing wrong, not by any logical measure. But the dictates of a lady's season are far from logical. It is one thing to be called a bluestocking, but to be spouting support for cats, and in such an unashamedly brazen fashion—"

"Brazen!"

One of the wolfhounds raised his head at Hannah's tone of sharp astonishment. He dropped it just as quickly, lapsing back into a snoring doze.

"In print, it is brazen, yes," Mattie said. "It's asserting your opinions as though they were on par with a man's. And like it or not, cats are associated with spinsters. The satirical magazines are forever pairing them together with comic drawings. If it becomes widely known that you have joined the ranks of cat-loving maidens, and in print, no less, people will remark on it. They live for such sport."

Hannah scoffed. "It is too much ridiculousness."

"It is the world we live in."

"Yes, but rational people—"

"Forget rational! You are on the marriage mart. Everything you say and do is weighed in the balance. A better friend would have taken that into consideration before printing your article. Indeed, *I* more than anyone should have known the danger. I know the high price of eccentricity."

Hannah listened to Mattie in growing disquiet. Was it true? Could people really be so smallminded? So judgmental? All because Hannah had dared to sign her full name to a printed article espousing basic kindness to animals?

"I am sorry," Mattie said. "I would undo it if I could."

"Can you not?"

"The journal has already been printed." Mattie set aside her teacup. She took a deep breath. "I am left with only two options. I can either send the journal to my subscribers as it is, or..."

"Or?"

"I can have the printer destroy the copies he's made. It would mean that there would be no issue this month."

"You could not simply have him make the correction?"

"He would have to reprint it," Mattie said. "And I can't afford the cost. My budget only stretches to one printing. Even that much is barely within my reach, and only because of the subscriptions people have taken."

Hannah frowned. She understood the repercussions. Still, she wasn't dissuaded by them. "You must send it out as is."

A horrified gasp escaped Ernsby from her place by the window.

Mattie leaned forward. "But Hannah—"

"You haven't many subscribers yet," Hannah said. "And those who have already bought subscriptions share our views. They will not be shocked to see my name in print, if they notice it at all."

"It isn't only my subscribers who have access to the *Animal Advocate*," Mattie said. "I received permission to distribute copies at the draper's in Milsom Street, and at the shop of a modiste I'm acquainted with in St. James's Parade.

Any of their customers can help themselves to a copy from the stack I leave on the counter."

Hannah was impressed rather than alarmed. "That is very enterprising of you."

A fleeting smile touched Mattie's lips. "One tries one's best." She at once grew serious again. "Of course, if I do go ahead with the issue, I can certainly refrain from giving away any copies this month."

"You needn't refrain," Hannah said. "Not on my account."

There was another gasp from Ernsby

"The risk to your reputation would be greater—" Mattie began.

"I know the risks," Hannah said, as much for her maid's benefit as for Mattie's. "But having strong beliefs means being strong enough to stand by them, no matter the cost."

Hannah's words did little to appease Ernsby. The lady's maid gave voice to her concerns the whole of the drive back to Camden Place.

"Everyone goes to that draper's shop," she said from her seat across from Hannah in the carriage. "Ladies and gentlemen alike, *and* their servants. It won't be a day or two after Miss Winthrop sets out those journals, or whatever you call 'em, before all of Bath knows your name and what you've allowed to be printed about yourself."

"Not about myself," Hannah replied. "About caring for one's cats."

"It *is* about yourself, miss. Everything a young lady does during her season reflects on her character."

"I hope it will," Hannah said stoutly. "There's nothing in that article that I wouldn't proclaim from the street corner if I thought people would listen."

Ernsby closed her eyes at this pronouncement, as though praying for divine intervention.

It was an overreaction, Hannah told herself. Nevertheless...

On returning to her parents' house, Hannah felt the faintest prickling of anxiety. Not because she regretted what she'd written, but because she suspected that Ernsby was right. The very act of having one's name in print was borderline scandalous for a young lady.

And worse.

Hannah now had someone else's opinion to consider. Someone who had only a few short weeks ago expressed justifiable misgivings about her ability to move in fashionable society. Someone who would now have verifiable proof that his suspicions had been proved right. If news should reach his ears...

What would James think?

Chapter Eighteen

The ballroom in Lord and Lady Teesdales' house near Lansdown Road was but a fraction of the size of the Carletons' ballroom. It was no less elegant. Hannah arrived on her brother's arm, clad in a gown of pale blue Marceline silk. Her parents had not come this evening. It wasn't considered fashionable for them to attend every event with her. Instead, it had fallen to Charles to escort her to the many dances, dinners, and concerts that comprised her season.

Charles professed not to mind it. However, anyone could see that he had been distracted of late with all the preparations for his marriage to Kate. While his betrothed was away in London purchasing her wedding clothes, he'd been obliged to remain in the West Country, not just for Hannah's sake but to settle affairs relating to Satterthwaite Court, the estate Hannah's parents had purchased for him in Devonshire.

Hannah's mother had grown up at Satterthwaite Court and had many fond memories of her childhood there.

When the property had recently come up for sale, Hannah's father had bought it with the intention of keeping it in the family. Charles and Kate were to live there now, a comfortable distance from both Heywood House and the Beresfords' Beasley Park.

"I'll have to travel there tomorrow," Charles said as they strolled along the crowded edge of the ballroom. "The estate agent wants to go over some of the repairs he's made to the upper rooms."

"Will you be obliged to stay overnight?" Hannah asked.

"I doubt it. Though I'm not likely to return in time to escort you to the concert at the Assembly Rooms."

"I don't mind missing it."

"You needn't," her brother said. "You can attend with Lady Carleton in my absence. She'll be happy to include you in her party."

Hannah's brow puckered. "Surely I have imposed on her ladyship enough this season."

"She doesn't view it as an imposition."

"Still... I would rather spend the evening catching up on my correspondence than being an awkward addition to someone else's party."

Charles gave her a look of concern. "You're not finding the season any more enjoyable?"

"There are parts of it I enjoy. The music. Sometimes the dancing."

"Sometimes?" he questioned.

"With the right partner," Hannah qualified.

A dance was in progress as they spoke. A lively reel, that had the couples skipping and spinning. Hannah's gaze lit on a familiar gentleman standing among the guests who had gathered to watch the dancers. "Oh look!" she said. "There's Jack!"

Catching sight of them in turn, Jack Beresford made his way through the crush. He smiled as he approached. "Heywood." He bowed to Charles before turning to Hannah. "Hannah. Don't you look fetching."

Hannah offered her hand to him in greeting. He took it, bowing over it with roguish gallantry.

"I daresay all your dances have been claimed in advance this evening," he said. "But if you have any to spare..." Retaining her hand, he helped himself to the dance card dangling from a cord at her wrist. He flipped through the pages with upraised brows. "What's this? Why so many empty spaces?"

"We've only just arrived," Hannah said.

"So have I." He relinquished her hand. "I've not seen him, by the way."

Hannah managed to contain her blushes. "I can't imagine who you mean."

Jack's eyes danced with humor. "Can you not?"

Charles gave Jack a repressive frown. He shook his head in silent warning. He knew how sensitive Hannah could be to teasing.

Jack's grin was unvanquished. "Shall we dance the next set?" he asked her.

"I'd like that," she said.

The instant the reel ended, Jack escorted her onto the floor. They lined up across from each other as the orchestra struck up the music for a sedate country dance.

"My esteemed elder brother is likely still toiling over his cravat," Jack said as they came together for the first turn. "He spends an egregious amount of time at his toilette. All that starch and finely pressed linen. While I, by contrast, have been blessed with effortless good looks."

Hannah bent her head at his unapologetic quizzing, both amused and embarrassed. "Is he not coming?" she asked, a little uncertain.

Jack's teasing smile softened as he turned her in a wide circle, their hands clasped and their arms extended. "He is," he said. "Indeed, he may well be here already. We don't travel together, you know."

They separated for a time. Hannah turned again on her own, stepping forward and back with the other dancers, before once again joining hands with Jack.

"Why did you come to Bath?" she asked him. "You weren't expected."

"I needed to talk to your brother," Jack said.

"What about?"

"Army business." He turned her in another wide circle. "Or rather, Navy business."

"You're not thinking of—"

"I am." He cocked a brow at her. "Do you disapprove?"

"No, but ...it *is* dangerous."

"I'm not afraid of a little danger."

"*Very* dangerous."

"A lot of danger, then." Jack promenaded down the line with her. "I've too much energy for Somerset. Too much, even, for London. What I need is a bit of adventure."

She flashed him a narrow look. "You sound like Charles did before he left home."

"Let me hazard a guess. You didn't like him joining up either."

"No, I didn't," she said frankly. "I know how it feels to

be left behind. When a gentleman goes away to war, it is dreadfully hard on his family."

"My family will soon grow accustomed to the idea," Jack said before they separated once more.

When they next came together, Hannah asked him, "What is it to be, then? The Army or the Navy?"

"I've not decided yet," he said. An expression of seriousness crossed his face. "I confess, the Naval stories that Charles has shared give me pause. For all its inconveniences, Her Majesty's Army is at least on dry land."

"You should speak with my father. He was in the cavalry for many years. Perhaps he could advise you?"

"Now why didn't I think of that?" Jack asked. He turned her again before they parted.

At the close of the set, he escorted her from the floor and back to her brother. Hannah's pulse quickened to find James standing with him, looking immaculate as ever. His cool gray gaze fell on her. The faintest shadow of a smile edged his mouth.

Her heart leapt in response to it. At the same time, she felt an overpowering trembling in her stomach, recalling the way he'd kissed her on the stairs of the Norman tower. The warmth of his lips. The unevenness of his breath. The way he'd held her so tightly, without art or finesse. The memory alone was enough to inspire a blush. This time she failed to suppress it.

"Miss Heywood." James bowed to her.

"Lord St. Clare." She curtsied to him in return.

Observing their formality, Jack grinned with gleeful amusement. "You're late," he said to his older brother. "You've missed the first set with her."

James's gaze remained on Hannah's face. "Perhaps she would be generous enough to grant me the next one?"

"I would be honored, my lord," Hannah replied.

"Heywood?" James briefly looked to Charles for permission.

"By all means," Charles said. "If my sister has no objection."

The orchestra was already beginning the first notes of a waltz as Hannah set her hand on James's sleeve and allowed him to lead her onto the floor. The trembling in her stomach increased, half anxiety and half anticipation. She had dreamed of waltzing with him again.

"How well you timed your arrival," she remarked as she stepped into his arms. "Just as you did at the Carletons' ball."

"It wasn't by design," he said. "I'd have been here earlier, but one of my horses came up lame. I went down to the Bull and Crown to have a look at him."

Her brow contracted with immediate concern. "Is he all right?"

"He strained his hock. It's nothing a few days' rest and a solicitously applied poultice won't cure."

"I'm glad to hear it," she said. "Glad you tended to him first."

"I was confident you would understand." James expertly led her into the first turn.

Hannah's breath caught, just as it had the last time they'd waltzed.

But no, she realized. It wasn't at all the same.

Then, she had been in awe of him. He had seemed almost godlike, too handsome and elegant to be partnered with a mere mortal like herself. On this occasion, however, Hannah knew them to be equals.

Her mouth curved in a dreamy smile as he waltzed her around the floor. The candlelight blurred about them, the flames shimmering in the ladies' colorful skirts and glinting in their jewels. It was magical. Romantic. Everything Hannah could have wished it to be.

"I must caution you," James said. "A compliment is forthcoming."

She was surprised into a laugh.

He stared down at her steadily. His gray eyes were warm. "Last time, you requested adequate warning."

Her cheeks heated under the weight of his gaze. "Very well. If you insist."

"You look beautiful this evening," he said.

Her smile of amusement faded. For all his absurdity, he was heart-meltingly serious.

He led her into another turn. Her silk skirts swirled about his legs. He was holding her so very close. "I don't often see you in blue," he said. "You're more often in some shade of pink or rose."

Hannah clutched his shoulder as he turned her again, temporarily rendered speechless. She was as amazed that he'd noticed her color preferences as she had been when he'd remembered the names of her dogs. "Do you not like shades of pink?" she asked when she at last found her voice.

"On the contrary," he said. "They suit you. Just as this shade does. I can't think of any color that wouldn't, lovely as you are."

Her eyes dropped to his chest as a wave of shyness engulfed her. "You are very generous with your compliments this evening."

"If it wouldn't make you uncomfortable, I would compliment you more lavishly still."

"It *would* make me uncomfortable," she said hastily, raising an anxious gaze back to his.

His hand curved around her waist, firm and strong, effortlessly guiding her through the crowd of dancers. "Then I'll keep my thoughts to myself," he said. "For now."

By the time the waltz came to a close, Hannah' nerve endings were quivering like a cat's whiskers, attuned to his every look and every touch.

Perhaps it had been dangerous to allow him to court her?

She might have known he would be magnificent at it. From his attentiveness and protectiveness, to the way he danced—the way he kissed. The way he had stepped in to rescue the donkey, for heaven's sake.

She was losing her heart to him.

Indeed, she very much feared she was falling in love with him.

And it *was* a fear, for despite her changing feelings for him, the obstacles that separated them were *un*changed.

"Shall we step outside for some air?" he asked her.

They were near the line of French doors that led onto the Teesdales' stone terrace.

Hannah cast a quick look about the ballroom for her brother. She couldn't find him. Still, she didn't think Charles would object. "Yes," she said. "Let's."

THE TEESDALES' TERRACE WAS MADE OF THE SAME honey-colored stone as most everything else in Bath. Illuminated by scattered torches, it spanned the back side of the house, facing south, several floors above an ornamental garden.

James escorted Hannah out. It was a cool evening, with the faint smell of spring roses drifting on the night air. Hannah dropped his arm as they walked together toward the terrace rail. She rested her hands upon the top of it, peering down into the garden below.

James stood back, watching her.

He hadn't been exaggerating when he'd told her how beautiful she looked this evening. *Or* when he'd said that she could do any color justice. He traced her profile with his gaze, seeing her more fully than he had on that fateful day when he'd proposed to her. There was no fault in her, not in her appearance, nor in her character, only softness and grace imbued to the very heart of her.

One could easily mistake that softness for weakness, particularly when coupled with her shyness and blushes. *He* had done so. He'd thought she required guidance, polishing, perfecting.

But she hadn't.

She didn't.

James could see that now. Just as he'd seen evidence of her strength, her confidence, her conscience. Qualities that were as striking as her beauty.

And yet, she wasn't some ideal to worship on a pedestal. She was a warm, and surprisingly passionate woman. One who had returned his kiss so sweetly that his heart still ached like the devil to recall it.

"It's such a perfectly manicured little garden," she remarked.

James came to stand beside her. "You don't like it?"

"I confess, I don't. The gardens at Heywood House are larger, and wilder. Like a fairytale garden one must cut through to save an enchanted princess."

His mouth quirked. "A vivid description."

There was an endless pause. "What are the gardens like at Worth House?" she asked.

James's gaze became intent. He studied her profile, attempting to discern the meaning behind her question. Was she generally curious about the Beresfords' family seat? Or was she specifically interested in it because she thought she might one day live there with him?

His pulse surged at the possibility.

He warned himself to tread carefully.

"Not as wild as the ones at Heywood House," he said. "But quite large and well established. We have a walled garden as well. It's shut up behind a wooden door twice as tall as a regular one. Only someone with a key can enter."

She continued looking down into the torchlit darkness, a shadow of a frown marring her brow.

He drew closer to her. "Worth House is at its best in the spring, when all the flowers are in bloom. There aren't many estates in Hertfordshire that can compete with its splendor."

"Will you retire there when you..."

"When I marry?"

She nodded.

No," he said. "Not while my father is living."

"Your father will live a good long while, I hope."

"I pray he will." Though James spent a great deal of

time thinking about the future, it was never pleasant to contemplate the melancholy event that would ultimately lead to him ascending to the title. "The earldom has other properties I might choose in the event of my marriage. If none of them suit, my parents have offered Beasley Park for my use. It is an easy distance from your family's estate."

Rather than being reassured by the information, she seemed to be troubled by it. "But you won't only reside in the country, will you? You said yourself that some of your life must be spent in town."

"So it must," James said.

Part of returning legitimacy to the Beresford name was developing a presence in London. It was incumbent on him to keep a hand in politics, and to nurture powerful connections. One day, he would be required to take his father's seat in the Lords. James would need to grow accustomed to remaining in town when Parliament was in session.

"How much of your life?" Hannah asked.

"Several months out of the year," he said.

"How many?"

James hesitated to answer. He knew very well what effect his reply would have. There was a good chance it would end their courtship before it had begun.

Even so, he couldn't bring himself to lie to her.

"Six, possibly," he said.

Chapter Nineteen

Hannah stared at James in the torchlight. "Six months!" she echoed in disbelief.

She was reminded of one of the myths she'd read as a girl. The one about Hades, God of the Underworld, and his stolen bride, Persephone. She too had ended up having to spend six-months of the year in a less than desirable residence. Although in Persephone's case, that residence was in hell, not in London.

At the moment, the two places didn't seem so vastly dissimilar. Not as far as Hannah was concerned. For a lady of a retiring temperament, one who struggled with meeting new people, and who could only find solace in the countryside with her animals, the notion of spending half the year in the most populous city in England, surrounded by judgmental elites, held a particular kind of horror.

She curled her fingers over the stone balustrade. "London is not a comfortable place for someone like myself."

James set his hand over hers. "Why not?"

Hannah felt the strength of him through his glove, a warm reassuring weight. A catch formed in her voice as she answered. "For the same reasons I told you when I rejected your proposal. To be alone in such a place, without family or friends, and to face the judgment of the beau monde, who make sport of anyone who is different—"

"You wouldn't be without family or friends," he said quietly. "If you came to London, you would be with me."

She flashed him a bleak look. "You would not wish to spend all your time looking after me."

"Would you require looking after?"

"No, but...perchance I would be lonely."

"Is that what you're afraid of?"

"I'm not afraid. I'm attempting to be realistic. Even the best husband cannot be with his wife always. She must necessarily take charge of her own sphere—the household, entertaining, appearing at society events and...and..."

James's fingers closed around hers, holding her hand safe in his. His voice deepened. "If you were mine, you would be my first and best concern. I would in all things endeavor to make you happy."

Hannah could think of no reply. She could only return his gaze, feeling for a moment as breathless as she'd felt when he swept her into the first turn of the waltz.

"I *could* make you happy," he said. "If you'll let me."

"I begin to believe you could," she said.

He stilled.

"It's all the rest that worries me," she said. "Thinking about what comes next."

"Don't think about it, then."

She smiled slightly. "And what should I be thinking about?"

"Us." He brought her hand to his lips. "This."

Her stomach fluttered.

"I've only begun to court you. There's time enough for all the rest of it." His thumb moved over her knuckles in a slow caress. "When can I see you again?"

Hannah's knees felt a trifle weak. It was dangerous to encourage him. To encourage *this*. Unless, of course, she truly wanted him for her own.

In that moment, she realized, for the first time, just how much she did.

"I'll be at home tomorrow," she said softly. "You would be very welcome to call if...if you'd like."

THE FOLLOWING AFTERNOON, HANNAH HAD several callers during her receiving hours. True to his word, James was one of them. He was the last to arrive, a fact which Hannah suspected was more by design than by happenstance. It allowed them to go for a walk rather than confine their visit to the formality of the drawing room.

She drew her cashmere shawl more firmly about her shoulders as they strolled through the Royal Victoria Park. Located at the end of Queen's Parade, it was a grassy, tree-studded sanctuary, replete with secluded walks and shady nooks where one could engage in private conversation. "Will you be attending the concert at the Assembly Rooms this evening?" she asked him.

James walked at her side. His dark wool frock coat was

open, revealing an exquisitely tailored shawl-collared blue waistcoat, and his tall hat was tipped down against the sun. "That depends," he said. "Will you be there?"

"I am to attend with Lady Carleton."

"Then, yes. I will."

She stifled a pleased smile. "It is to be in Italian. And very beautiful too, I'm told, even if one doesn't speak the language."

"If you'll permit me to sit beside you, I shall be happy to provide a translation."

Her cheeks glowed. "I will save you a seat, of course."

A smile edged James's mouth. "How else have you been occupying your time since last I saw you?" he asked. "Aside from entertaining callers."

"There have not been so many of those. Indeed, it's my correspondence that's taken up the bulk of my free time. I've fallen terribly behind since the start of my season."

"Ah, yes. As I recall, you're a capital letter writer."

"I am," she said, on her mettle. "At least, I *was* before having to devote so many hours to balls and concerts and the like." She adjusted her shawl. "I had a letter just this morning from my friend, Miss Winthrop."

"The publisher of the *Animal Advocate*?" James asked, looking at her.

Hannah warmed under his regard. One of the things she liked best about him was that he didn't affect a polite curiosity about the subjects that meant something to her. Whenever she spoke, he showed a genuine interest. And he listened. *Really* listened. "She has become a good friend since I arrived in Bath."

"I look forward to making her acquaintance."

"I hope you shall, in time." Hannah hesitated. "Did I

mention that she's agreed to publish my cat article? Indeed, she *has* published it. The new journal went out to its subscribers several days ago."

"Which makes you a multipublished author?" James smiled. "I congratulate you."

Two riders trotted by along the avenue. One of the men touched his hat to them in acknowledgment as he and his companion passed. James inclined his head in return.

It was a lovely day out, and there were several people in the park taking advantage of it. Mothers and their children, nurses and invalids, and even a few couples like Hannah and James.

"You're not scandalized by the fact?" she asked him.

"Should I be?"

"You might be," she said.

James gave her another look.

Hannah was steeling herself to explain about her name being printed in the *Animal Advocate* when she heard a faint, but entirely distinctive, noise emanating from a patch of woodland that ran alongside the path. She came to an abrupt halt. "Is that...?"

James stopped alongside her as the noise came again. "It sounds like a kitten."

"Several kittens," Hannah said. There was no mistaking the plaintive cries. She entered the stand of trees, moving toward the sound with a cautious step. She didn't wish to startle the poor creatures. Unless she was mistaken, they were in distress. Either hurt or hungry.

Or worse.

James followed her, just in time to see a man hunched over the underbrush. He held a burlap sack in one beefy hand and a struggling gray kitten in the other.

Outrage rose in Hannah's breast. "I beg your pardon, sir!" She strode toward the man. "Just what is it you think you're doing?"

The man straightened. Dressed in brown homespun and a tweed cap, he had the look of a groundskeeper or gamekeeper. He kept hold of the kitten's scruff, ignoring its cries as it thrashed in his grasp. "What someone shoulda done days ago," he said. "Disposing of these creatures to save 'em from suffering."

There were three more kittens huddled in the undergrowth—all of them varying shades of gray, and all of them crying pitifully. They couldn't have been more than four weeks old.

"Where is their mother?" Hannah asked.

"Dead," the man said. "And they ain't old enough to fend for themselves."

Hannah's kindling gaze flashed from the kitten in the man's right hand to the burlap sack in his left. "You surely aren't going to drown them?"

"Best thing for 'em," the man said. "It's a kindness."

James came to stand beside Hannah. She was certain she heard him utter a weary sigh. "I think not," he said.

The groundskeeper gave a visible start at James's tone of authority. "Sir?"

"Relinquish the kitten," James said. "We shall take charge of him—and the others."

Hannah was already slipping off her shawl. The kittens appeared quite wild. She had no wish to alarm them any further than was necessary. She scooped up the kitten that dangled from the groundskeeper's fingers an instant before the man released it.

The kitten didn't willingly accept his rescue. He uttered

a menacing growl, as sinister as the buzzing of an enraged bee. His little body thrashed within the confines of the soft cashmere.

Hannah pressed the precious bundle close to her, murmuring soothing words. She was vaguely aware of James exchanging words with the groundskeeper. He gave the man a coin before sending him off.

"I presume you know how to feed kittens of this age," James said after the man had gone.

"I do," Hannah assured him. She would soak a soft cloth in warm milk and allow the kittens to nurse from it. It would do until they could be persuaded to take solid food.

James crouched beside the three remaining kittens. "Do you want them all in your shawl?"

"Yes, but you mustn't—"

Before she could complete her warning, James made the grievous error of gathering the kittens up with his hands.

Hannah gave an eloquent wince as, before her eyes, the three small kittens were transformed into a hissing and spitting ball of feline mayhem. They clawed at James wildly, one climbing up his waistcoat, the other snapping its teeth at his hands, and the third striking out with its claws.

"Bloody hell," James muttered under his breath as the smallest kitten scratched his face. A line of blood welled across his cheek.

"Oh, do have a care!" Hannah hurried toward him, opening her shawl. "Put them in here with their brother before they tear you to ribbons."

"I'm all right," James said. He gently pried the kittens from his waistcoat, placing them into her shawl one at a time, even as a droplet of blood slid down his jaw untended. "Poor mites. They're frightened, that's all."

Hannah's heart thumped heavily as she gazed up at him. Whatever doubt she'd had about their future together slipped away. And just like that, standing there in Victoria Park, a bundle of squirming kittens clutched to her breast, she fell all of the way in love with him.

Chapter Twenty

"What the devil happened to you?" Jack asked.

James walked past him on his way down to the kitchens. He held his handkerchief to his cheek. "A minor mishap."

Jack followed after him. There was a periodical folded in his hand. "Is that *blood?*"

"A kitten scratch."

"A kitten climbed up your *face?* Good God, don't tell me. Hannah Heywood was somehow involved."

James ignored his brother. Entering the kitchen, he signaled to the cook. She was alone in front of the fire, drinking a cup of tea. "I require a pot of salve," he said. "And a plaster wouldn't go amiss."

Cook was immediately on her feet. "Right away, my lord." She bobbed a curtsy before disappearing into the store cupboard.

"The timing couldn't be worse," Jack said. "Considering what's transpired."

James went to the sink. He wet his handkerchief at the

tap. Wringing it out, he again brought it to his cheek. "What is it you're muttering about?"

"I was at the Pump Room this morning, talking with Colonel Jensen about the possibility of joining his regiment, when I saw Lord Fennick huddled with Miss Paley and several others. I heard one of them mention—"

Cook returned before Jack could finish his story. She unscrewed the lid from a small jar of salve as she approached. "Might I have a look at it, sir?"

James dutifully removed his handkerchief, revealing the scratch on his cheek. "Courtesy of a very small cat," he informed her.

"Dirty beasts," Cook said as she inspected the wound. "But it should heal up right enough, so long as you keep it clean." She motioned to one of the chairs at the plank table. "Sit down, my lord, if you please. I'll tend to it."

James obeyed her. Taking a seat, he waited while she cleaned and treated the scratch, and then covered it with a sticking plaster.

Jack hovered nearby. "Can you give us a moment?" he asked when she'd finished.

Cook collected the salve and the remains of her nursing kit. She bobbed another curtsy before slipping out the door. It was well past luncheon and many hours yet until dinner. In the Cook's absence, the kitchen temporarily stood empty, with no sign of any footmen or scullery maids to interrupt them.

"What's that you're brandishing about?" James asked his brother, irritated.

Jack tossed the folded periodical to him across the table. "See for yourself."

James picked it up. It was a thin journal, neatly bound,

with its name printed across the cover: *The Animal Advocate*. He lifted his gaze. "Where did you get this?"

"It was one of several dozen, stacked high on the counter at the draper's shop in Milsom Street. They're giving them away to anyone who wants a copy." Jack's expression was uncharacteristically sober. "You'll find Hannah's contribution on page sixteen."

James flipped through the pages until he found it—a brief essay illustrated with a drawing of a cat eating from a small, flat dish. He scanned Hannah's words. On reading them, his first reaction was one of pride. She wrote with eloquence and economy, getting straight to the heart of the matter. She also employed compassion in her argument. He would have expected nothing less.

"What of it?" he asked.

"You're not alarmed?"

"That she's contributed to an animal welfare journal? No."

"That she's used her full name." Jack tapped his finger on a line of small print below the essay's title.

James's eyes followed. He hadn't noticed it at first glance, but the attribution jumped out at him now so boldly—so blatantly—that it might have been emblazoned across the sky.

"Written by Miss Hannah Heywood," Jack said grimly. "How many Hannah Heywoods are there in the West Country, I wonder? Only one, I'd guess. And so has everyone else who has read her name here, Fennick included."

James slowly set down the journal and met his brother's gaze. "What about Fennick?"

"That's how I knew to look at the draper's shop," Jack

said. "That blackguard and his cronies were bandying about Hannah's name at the Pump Room."

James's blood simmered with fury. "Were they."

"Had I not been with Colonel Jensen, I would have done something about it there and then. Indeed, I should have done. Fennick was making her a figure of fun. He was laughing at her."

Laughing at Hannah?

No longer simmering, James's blood swiftly rose to a raging boil. He stood from the table. "Where is he now?"

Jack took a step back. Something he saw in James's face made his own face lose its color. "He and the others went into Kelston for the afternoon. I heard him say he wouldn't be returning until this evening. He plans to attend the concert at the Assembly Rooms."

"How fortuitous," James said. "So do I."

* * *

James arrived at the Assembly Rooms that evening to find Lord Fennick standing with a small group of acquaintances by one of the four fireplaces in the Octagon Room. Several other ladies and gentlemen were similarly disposed throughout the room. Hannah wasn't among them.

"You're not going to cause a scene, I trust," Jack said, following in James's wake as he crossed the floor toward Fennick.

James's gaze was fixed on his former schoolmate. "I shouldn't think it likely."

"Nor would I," Jack said under his breath, "in normal circumstances."

Fennick turned his head as they approached. He was dressed in elegant eveningwear, his hair and mustache pomaded into meticulous order. Seeing James, his mouth curved into a smug smile. "St. Clare."

Two of the ladies in Fennick's party joined him in staring at James. One of them was Miss Paley.

"Lord St. Clare!" she exclaimed. "I hoped we might have the pleasure of seeing you here."

James acknowledged the ladies with a stiff bow, his attention never straying from his quarry. "A word, Fennick," he said.

Fennick's face glimmered with suppressed mirth. He addressed the ladies and gentlemen in his party: "If you will excuse me?"

Miss Paley and the others followed him with their eyes as he strolled away to join James.

"You have something to say to me?" Fennick asked.

James faced him. His temper had cooled only slightly since Jack's revelations in the kitchen. *Very* slightly. Anger still kindled within him—hot and unpredictable. It wouldn't take much to bring it back into full flame. "I warned you," he said.

Fennick's mouth curled wider. "Warned me about what?"

"About whom," Jack corrected from his place beside James.

Fennick snorted. "Who are you meant to be? His second?"

"An exceedingly interested bystander," Jack shot back. "I've been waiting to witness this moment my entire life."

James ignored his brother. "I told you not to mention her name," he said to Fennick.

"I presume you're speaking of Miss Heywood?"

"I am."

"And just what is it you're accusing me of?"

James didn't hesitate. "Of being an ungentlemanly lout."

Fennick's smile turned brittle. "Ungentlemanly? That's something, coming from you." He moved closer to James. "And you wonder why I dislike you?"

"I don't wonder at all," James said.

"All those years at school, acting as though you were better than the rest of us. And all the while you were nothing more than the son of a known—"

"Say it," James said quietly, "and I'll smash your teeth down your throat."

Fennick gave another derisive snort. "You wouldn't dare. Just as you didn't at Oxford. Always the man of restraint. Butter wouldn't melt. And now you've set your sights on Miss Heywood. A bluestocking, I've discovered, with a keen affection for cats." He chuckled. "Well, water finds its own level, I'm told. You the son of a bastard and Miss Heywood a—"

James punched him in the face.

HANNAH ENTERED THE OCTAGON ROOM IN company with Lady Carleton in time to witness what appeared to be a brawl. A circle of bystanders had gathered around two coatless gentlemen who were going at each other with unchecked ferocity. It took Hannah a full five seconds to realize that one of those men was James.

All signs of his famously icy control had fled. His golden hair was disheveled, and blood trickled from the edge of his mouth. He exchanged blows with Fennick, trading him punch for punch, each punishing strike punctuated by the sickening sound of bare knuckles on flesh and bone.

Alarm swept through her.

"Good heavens!" Abandoning her chaperone, Hannah rushed toward the fight. She pushed through the assembled throng, all of whom were looking on with expressions of mingled horror and delight.

Jack stood on the inside of the circle. He wasn't attempting to stop the altercation. On the contrary. He was offering muttered words of encouragement to his older brother. "Like that. And again. That's it. Show him no mercy."

Hannah grasped hold of his sleeve. "Jack! What in the world is going on?"

Jack's gaze jolted to hers. His eyes went round with surprise. "Hannah!"

Hearing her name, James jerked his head to look at her.

Lord Fennick took the opportunity to deliver a punishing blow to the side of James's jaw.

"Oh!" Hannah cried. "How could you?" Heedless of the danger in coming between them, she flew to James's side. She brought her hands to tenderly cradle his face, even as she scowled at Fennick. "Is that what you call honorable, sir?"

Fennick's nose was bleeding and one of his eyes was swollen half shut. His hair hung limply over his forehead.

He looked altogether worse than James. "It wasn't I who struck the first blow, ma'am," he said rigidly.

"Whoever started the quarrel is irrelevant," Lady Carleton pronounced, coming to join them. "It has gone on quite long enough." She glared first at Fennick and then at James. "Shame on the pair of you. There are ladies present." Her gaze swept over the crowd. "And shame on the rest of you. Any one of you gentlemen could have broken this up at the onset. Instead, you've stood by, gawping, as though you were enjoying a match in a boxing saloon."

The gentlemen sheepishly murmured their regrets before dispersing along with the ladies.

"My apologies, my lady," James said. "Miss Heywood."

Hannah required no apology. She continued gently examining James's face for injuries. In addition to the blood and bruising he'd received from his fight, he had another wound to add to his tally. There was a plaster on his cheek in the place where the kitten had scratched him. Seeing it, her heart swelled with love for him.

"I beg your pardon, your ladyship. Miss Heywood." Fennick gave a stilted bow. "If you will excuse me."

Jack watched him go with an expression of satisfaction. "You made mincemeat out of him," he remarked to James.

"That is sufficient commentary from you, Mr. Beresford," Lady Carleton snapped. And then to James. "Remove yourself, my lord. You are in no state to attend the concert."

"Yes, ma'am," James said.

Hannah's hands slid to the front of his waistcoat. "I'll go with you."

James's countenance softened as he looked at her. "No."

He covered her hand with his. "I appreciate the sentiment, but it wouldn't be proper."

"Propriety fled some time ago, sir," Lady Carleton said dryly. "See him home, Miss Heywood, if that is what you wish. You may use my carriage."

Chapter Twenty-One

"Why did you fight him?" Hannah asked. She and James were seated side-by-side in Lady Carleton's luxurious, velvet-upholstered carriage as the driver guided the horses at a leisurely walk over the cobblestones. The carriage lamps were lit, casting a faint glow over the darkened interior of the cab.

"I shouldn't have," James said as Hannah applied her handkerchief to the edge of his lip. His mouth was set in a pensive frown, his gray eyes watchful. He'd been studying her face ever since they left the Octagon Room, seeming to be gauging the measure of her reaction to the altercation she'd just witnessed.

"No, indeed," she said, dabbing at the blood. "Not at the Assembly Rooms, at any rate." She paused before softly asking again. "Why did you?"

"Because he deserved it," James replied gruffly. "And because...I'd had enough."

Hannah met his eyes with slow dawning understanding. "He said something about your family?"

"After a fashion." His frown deepened. For a moment, it seemed he wouldn't expound on his answer. And then: "He made a comment about your cat article."

Hannah lowered her hand from his face. Her handkerchief remained clutched limply in her fingers. "Lord Fennick read my article?"

"The animal journal was at the draper's shop, apparently. Jack says they were giving them away."

Hannah nodded. "Miss Winthrop distributes copies there. It helps her to get the word out."

"She's succeeded. Fennick saw it, along with Miss Paley and their friends. He took the opportunity to remark on it, after I'd explicitly warned him that he wasn't to mention your name."

She stilled. This was news to her. "Why ever would you have issued such a warning?"

"Fennick and I have been at odds since university," James said. "If he thought for a moment that he could get to me by hurting you, he wouldn't hesitate to do it. And I won't permit him, or anyone, to hurt you. Not ever. Not even if I must make a thorough spectacle of myself."

Guilt assailed her. However tender the sentiment in his words, the meaning was the same. He'd lost control because of her. He'd subjected himself to scandal. No wonder he was looking so grim, so unrelentingly somber. He must have at last realized the price of any connection with someone as eccentric as herself.

"This is my fault," she said. "If I hadn't exposed myself to ridicule, you would never have felt obliged to fight with Lord Fennick. And now you're upset with me—"

"I'm not upset with you," he said.

She looked up at him anxiously.

"I'm angry with myself," he said. "All this time, I've been so bloody careful, trying to convince you that you can trust me with your heart. I had hoped that, after this evening, you might be close to changing your mind about me. Instead, all I've done is provide you with incontrovertible evidence of my true character."

Some of the tension eased out of her. "Yes. I suppose you have." She brought her handkerchief back to his lip, pressing it gently against his wound.

His eyes met hers with rueful humor. "I've wanted to pummel Fennick since my first year at Oxford. I never succumbed to the impulse, despite ample provocation. Not until tonight. And then...God help me. I couldn't seem to stop myself."

"I can well understand it."

"Can you?"

"Naturally," she said. "One will go to extraordinary lengths to defend someone they love."

James stared down at her. He didn't speak.

Hannah felt a scalding blush rising in her cheeks. But she wasn't ashamed to have mentioned it, even if she must be the one to mention it first. "You do love me, don't you?" she asked.

"More than life," he said.

Her vision clouded with tears

He covered her hand with his, drawing it to his chest. He held it there against the heavy beat of his heart. "I believe I've loved you since the night I encountered you in the Beasley Park stables," he said. "I knew then how very special you were—how very essential to my happiness. But it's *your* happiness I've come to care about, not mine. If you don't return my feelings—"

"Oh, but I do," she said in an earnest rush. She leaned into him. "I do love you, James, so very, very much."

His solemn expression fractured. It seemed to her that, for a breathless moment, his eyes shimmered too. And then, his arms came about her and his mouth seized hers, kissing her fiercely, sweetly.

She encircled his neck, kissing him back.

"You don't have to accompany me to London," he said several scorching moments later. "So long as you're mine, and so long as I know you're waiting when I return—"

"Of course I'll accompany you," Hannah said.

She understood him now. Knew that he needed her to stand beside him. Not as a hollow trophy, or as some flawless approximation of a society wife, but as an ally. A partner. Someone to fight for him and defend him, just as Hannah would do for anyone else she loved.

"There's no question of that," she said "Not anymore." She paused. "I've only one condition."

"Anything."

"You must ask me again that question you asked in my parents' drawing room that day."

He bent his head to hers. His voice deepened on a husky confession. "I'm afraid to ask it."

Hannah smiled. She smoothed the hair at his nape. "You? Afraid? I don't believe it."

His mouth hitched with wry humor. "I promised your father that if you rejected me again, I would leave Bath never to return."

Her brows shot up. "Papa made you promise *that*?"

"He did," James said. "You can see why I've been reluctant to frighten you off."

"There's no fear of that. Not anymore." She prompted him softly, "Ask me, James."

He drew back just enough to meet her eyes. The carriage lamp shone over his face, no longer merely handsome, but infinitely dear. "Will you marry me, sweetheart?"

Hannah returned his gaze as the carriage rolled steadily toward Camden Place. Her eyes blurred again, even as her heart brimmed over with love for him. She had long thought him perfect. Now she knew, beyond all doubt, that he was perfect for her.

"Yes," she said. "I will."

Epilogue

J ames and Hannah's engagement was celebrated the following afternoon with a small party at the Heywoods' house in Camden Place. Hannah's parents were in attendance, along with Charles, Jack, the Carletons, and Hannah's friend, Miss Winthrop. None of them remarked on the bruises James sported on his face, nor on the events of last evening (except for Jack, who admitted to having written Ivo with a gleeful report of James's public brawl).

After several champagne toasts and a few happy tears on the part of Mrs. Heywood, Lady Carleton, and even Miss Winthrop, James found his way to the edge of the drawing room where Captain Heywood stood, with the aid of his cane. His usually stern expression was softened with affection as he regarded his wife and daughter.

They were seated together on the sofa. Mrs. Heywood was smiling, her arm around Hannah in a loving embrace as Hannah held out her slim hand for the ladies to admire her engagement ring. James had purchased it for her only that morning at a jeweler in Northumberland Place. A fine rose-cut diamond, as flawless as Hannah was herself.

Nearby, Jack sat in close conversation with Charles and Lord Carleton, discussing the Army or the Navy, no doubt. He was still hellbent on joining up. Thus far nothing—and no one—had managed to dissuade him.

"You've made my daughter very happy," the captain said as James joined him.

James followed his gaze to Hannah. Her beautiful face was aglow with smiles and blushes. The sight of it provoked a similar glow within him. "She's made me exceedingly happy as well," he said. "I love her, sir."

"I can well believe it." Captain Heywood glanced at him. "You wired your parents?"

"First thing this morning." James expected they'd be having another celebration soon in grand Beresford style. His mother would see to it. Indeed, given Ivo and Kate's impending marriages, the next year would likely be one long celebration, filled with wedding parties, honeymoons, and endless toasts to the various couples' health and happiness.

"They'll be pleased?" the captain asked.

"Delighted," James said. "Both of my parents encouraged the match."

Captain Heywood didn't appear surprised. "My daughter is a great prize."

"She is," James agreed, looking at Hannah. He still couldn't believe she'd said yes. That she loved him, as he loved her.

"Her mother has been the making of me," Captain Heywood said.

"My father would very likely say the same about his marriage to my mother."

"You'll benefit from his advice."

"And yours too, I hope."

"My advice is to love her. To listen to her. And to take every care that her compassionate heart is never constrained by an excess of propriety."

"In other words," James said, "let her bring home as many donkeys, dogs, and kittens as she pleases."

The captain's eyes twinkled with wry humor. "In short, yes."

Hannah caught James's gaze from across the drawing room. Her mouth curved in a slow smile. James's chest tightened in reply. She didn't have to beckon to him. His soul was drawn inexorably to her warmth, just as it had been since the first moment they'd met.

"If you'll excuse me," he said to Captain Heywood.

This time, the captain smiled too. "By all means."

Author's Note

Hannah Heywood's support for the burgeoning animal welfare movement is based in historical fact. The nineteenth century was a time of dramatic change in terms of how British society viewed the treatment of animals, whether those animals were house pets, carriage horses, or animals in laboratories. The Royal Society for the Prevention of Cruelty to Animals was founded in 1824, with Princess Victoria (soon to be Queen Victoria) named as its patron in 1835. It was the first animal welfare charity in the world, and a tangible reflection of the public's changing attitudes.

As a character, Hannah embodies these more compassionate views, both in her actions on behalf of animals and in the way she lives her life. Her refusal to eat meat is also based in historical fact. Vegetarianism in the Victorian era wasn't unique. As a lifestyle, it was often associated with cultural reform movements, including animal welfare reform and the antivivisection movement. The first vegetarian society in England would be formed in 1847, just a few short years after the setting of this novel.

When writing *A Lady of Conscience*, I also drew inspiration from an 1856 court case involving a stolen pet donkey. The donkey—a handsome fellow, named Tuppy—was the much-cherished pet of a farmer's daughter. Stolen from his home, Tuppy was discovered five years later, pulling a costermonger's cart in London. Encountering the little donkey on the street, the farmer's daughter recognized him at once. She brought the costermonger to court, demanding the return of her former pet.

You can read more about this case in my nonfiction book *The Pug Who Bit Napoleon: Animal Tales of the 18th and 19th Centuries*.

Finally, a few words on historical language. In my Somerset Stories series, the English county name of Somerset is sometimes used interchangeably with Somersetshire. Somersetshire is the historical name for Somerset and was used fairly commonly in the region during the Regency and early Victorian period, and in many publications of the eighteenth and nineteenth centuries.

Acknowledgments

This book came at a difficult time for me. Midway through writing it, I had a health setback. It meant that I finished the story in a lot of pain. If it wasn't for the support, encouragement, and assistance of the wonderful people around me, it's very possible I wouldn't have finished it at all. Many thanks to my amazing assistant Rel Mollet; to my brilliant agent Kevan Lyon; to Kathryn Stuart, my very patient editor at Audible; to James Egan for cover design; and to Flora for beta reading.

Thanks, love, and gratitude are also due to my marvelous mom, who read this book over and over again, with every revision. And to my devoted menagerie—Stella, Jet, Tavi, Bijou, and Asteria—who lent their moral support as I wrote.

Last but never least, I'd like to thank you, my readers. I'm so grateful to you for sticking with me, and with this series. These second-generation stories are entirely for you!

An Excerpt from The Matrimonial Advertisement

Read on for a Sneak Peek into *The Matrimonial Advertisement*, one of Mimi's most beloved stories and the first book in her Parish Orphans of Devon series.

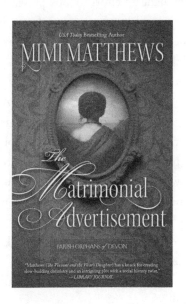

PROLOGUE

North Devon, England
September 1859

Helena Reynolds crossed the floor of the crowded taproom, her carpetbag clutched in her trembling hands. The King's Arms was only a small coaching inn on the North Devon coast road, but it seemed to her as if every man in Christendom had gathered there to have a pint. She could feel their eyes on her as she navigated carefully through their midst. Some stares were merely curious. Others were openly assessing.

She suppressed a shiver. She was hardly dressed for seduction in her gray striped-silk traveling gown, though she'd certainly made an effort to look presentable. After all, it was not every day that one met one's future husband.

"Can I help you, ma'am?" the innkeeper called to her from behind the crowded bar.

"Yes. If you please, sir." Tightening her hands on her carpetbag, she approached the high counter. A very tall man was leaning against the end of it, nursing his drink. His lean, muscular frame was shrouded in a dark wool greatcoat, his face partially hidden by his upturned collar and a tall beaver hat tipped low over his brow. She squeezed into the empty space beside him, her heavy petticoats and crinoline rustling loudly as they pressed against his leg.

She lowered her voice to address the innkeeper directly. "I'm here to see—"

"Blevins!" a man across the room shouted. "Give us another round!"

Before Helena could object, the innkeeper darted off to oblige his customers. She stared after him in helpless frustration. She'd been expected at one o'clock precisely. And now, after the mix-up at the railway station and the delay with the accommodation coach—she cast an anxious glance at the small watch she wore pinned to the front of her bodice—it was already a quarter past two.

"Sir!" she called to the innkeeper. She stood up on the toes of her half boots, trying to catch his eye. "Sir!"

He did not acknowledge her. He was exchanging words with the coachman at the other end of the counter as he filled five tankards with ale. The two of them were laughing together with the ease of old friends.

Helena gave a soft huff of annoyance. She was accustomed to being ignored, but this was the outside of enough. Her whole life hinged on the next few moments.

She looked around for someone who might assist her. Her eyes fell at once on the gentleman at her side. He didn't appear to be a particularly friendly sort of fellow, but his height was truly commanding and surely he must have a voice to match his size.

"I beg your pardon, sir." She touched him lightly on the arm with one gloved hand. His muscles tensed beneath her fingers. "I'm sorry to disturb you, but would you mind very much to summon—"

He raised his head from drinking and, very slowly, turned to look at her.

The words died on Helena's lips.

He was burned. Badly burned.

"Do you require something of me, ma'am?" he asked in an excruciatingly civil undertone.

She stared up at him, her first impression of his

appearance revising itself by the second. The burns, though severe, were limited to the bottom right side of his face, tracing a path from his cheek down to the edge of his collar and beyond it, she was sure. The rest of his face—a stern face with a strongly chiseled jaw and hawklike aquiline nose—was relatively unmarked. Not only unmarked, but with his black hair and smoke-gray eyes, actually quite devastatingly handsome.

"Do you require something of me?" he asked again, more sharply this time.

She blinked. "Yes. Do forgive me. Would you mind very much summoning the innkeeper? I cannot seem to—"

"*Blevins!*" the gentleman bellowed.

The innkeeper broke off his loud conversation and scurried back to their end of the counter. "What's that, guv?"

"The lady wishes to speak with you."

"Thank you, sir," Helena said. But the gentleman had already turned his attention back to his drink, dismissing her without a word.

"Yes, ma'am?" the innkeeper prompted.

Abandoning all thoughts of the handsome—and rather rude—stranger at her side, Helena once again addressed herself to the innkeeper. "I was supposed to meet someone here at one o'clock. A Mr. Boothroyd?" She felt the gentleman next to her stiffen, but she did not regard it. "Is he still here?"

"Another one for Boothroyd, are you?" The innkeeper looked her up and down. "Don't look much like the others."

Helena's face fell. "Oh?" she asked faintly. "Have there been others?"

"Aye. Boothroyd's with the last one now."

"The *last* one?" She couldn't believe it. Mr. Boothroyd had given her the impression that she was the only woman with whom Mr. Thornhill was corresponding. And even if she wasn't, what sort of man interviewed potential wives for his employer in the same manner one might interview applicants for a position as a maidservant or a cook? It struck her as being in extraordinarily bad taste.

Was Mr. Thornhill aware of what his steward was doing?

She pushed the thought to the back of her mind. It was far too late for doubts. "As that may be, sir, I've come a very long way and I'm certain Mr. Boothroyd will wish to see me."

In fact, she was not at all certain. She had only ever met Mr. Finchley, the sympathetic young attorney in London. It was he who had encouraged her to come to Devon. While the sole interaction she'd had with Mr. Boothroyd and Mr. Thornhill thus far were letters—letters which she currently had safely folded within the contents of her carpetbag.

"Reckon he might at that," the innkeeper mused.

"Precisely. Now, if you'll inform Mr. Boothroyd I've arrived, I would be very much obliged to you."

The man beside her finished his ale in one swallow and then slammed the tankard down on the counter. "I'll take her to Boothroyd."

Helena watched, wide-eyed, as he stood to his full, towering height. When he glared down at her, she offered him a tentative smile. "I must thank you again, sir. You've been very kind."

He glowered. "This way." And then, without a backward glance, he strode toward the hall.

Clutching her carpetbag tightly, she trotted after him. Her heart was skittering, her pulse pounding in her ears. She prayed she wouldn't faint before she'd even submitted to her interview.

The gentleman rapped once on the door to the private parlor. It was opened by a little gray-haired man in spectacles. He peered up at the gentleman, frowned, and then, with furrowed brow, looked past him to stare at Helena herself.

"Mr. Boothroyd?" she queried.

"I am Boothroyd," he said. "And you, I presume, are Miss Reynolds?"

"Yes, sir. I know I'm dreadfully late for my appointment..." She saw a woman rising from a chair within the private parlor. A woman who regarded Helena with an upraised chin, her face conveying what words could not. "Oh," Helena whispered. And just like that it seemed the tiny, flickering flame of hope she'd nurtured these last months blinked out. "You've already found someone else."

"As to that, Miss Reynolds—" Mr. Boothroyd broke off with an expression of dismay as the tall gentleman brushed past him to enter the private parlor. He removed his hat and coat and proceeded to take a seat by the raging fire in the hearth.

The woman gaped at him in dismay. "Mr. Boothroyd!" she hissed, hurrying to the older gentleman's side. "I thought this was a *private* parlor."

"So it is, Mrs. Standish." Mr. Boothroyd consulted his pocket watch. "Or was, until half an hour ago. Never mind it. Our interview is finished in any case. Now, if you would be so good as to..."

Helena didn't hear the rest of their conversation. All she

could hear was the sound of her own beating heart. She didn't know why she remained. She'd have to board the coach and continue to Cornwall. And then what? Fling herself from the cliffs, she supposed. There was no other way. Oh, what a fool she'd been to think this would work in the first place! If only Jenny had never seen that advertisement in the paper. Then she would have known months ago that there was but one means of escape from this wretched tangle. She would never have had reason to hope!

Her vision clouded with tears. She turned from the private parlor, mumbling an apology to Mr. Boothroyd as she went.

"Miss Reynolds?" Mr. Boothroyd called. "Have you changed your mind?"

She looked back, confused, only to see that the other lady was gone and that Mr. Boothroyd stood alone in the entryway. From his seat by the fire, the tall gentleman ruffled a newspaper, seeming to be wholly unconcerned with either of them. "No, sir," she said.

"If you will have a seat." He gestured to one of the chairs that surrounded a small supper table. On the table was a stack of papers and various writing implements. She watched him rifle through them as she took a seat. "I trust you had a tolerable journey."

"Yes, thank you."

"You took the train from London?"

"I did, sir, but only as far as Barnstaple. Mr. Finchley arranged for passage on an accommodation coach to bring me the rest of the way here. It's one of the reasons I'm late. There was an overturned curricle in the road. The coachman stopped to assist the driver."

"One of the reasons, you say?"

"Yes, I...I missed the earlier train at the station," she confessed. "I'd been waiting at the wrong platform and...by the time I realized my error, my train had already gone. I was obliged to change my ticket and take the next one."

"Have you no maid with you? No traveling companion?"

"No, sir. I traveled alone." There hadn't been much choice. Jenny had to remain in London, to conceal Helena's absence as long as possible. Helena had considered hiring someone to accompany her, but there'd been no time and precious little money to spare. Besides which, she didn't know who she could trust.

Mr. Boothroyd continued to sift through his papers. Helena wondered if he was even listening to her. "Ah. Here it is," he said at last. "Your initial reply to the advertisement." He withdrew a letter covered in small, even handwriting which she recognized as her own. "As well as a letter from Mr. Finchley in London with whom you met on the fifteenth." He perused a second missive with a frown.

"Is anything the matter?" she asked.

"Indeed. It says here that you are five and twenty." Mr. Boothroyd lowered the letter. "You do not look five and twenty, Miss Reynolds."

"I assure you that I am, sir." She began to work at the ribbons of her gray silk traveling bonnet. After untying the knot with unsteady fingers, she lifted it from her head, twined the ribbons round it, and placed it atop her carpetbag. When she raised her eyes, she found Mr. Boothroyd staring at her. "I always look much younger in a bonnet. But, as you can see now, I'm—"

"Young *and* beautiful," he muttered with disapproval.

She blushed, glancing nervously at the gentleman by the fire. He did not seem to be listening, thank goodness. Even so, she leaned forward in her chair, dropping her voice. "Does Mr. Thornhill not want a pretty wife?"

"This isn't London, Miss Reynolds. Mr. Thornhill's house is isolated. Lonely. He seeks a wife who can bear the solitude. Who can manage his home and see to his comforts. A sturdy, capable sort of woman. Which is precisely why the advertisement specified a preference for a widow or spinster of more mature years."

"Yes, but I—"

"What Mr. Thornhill doesn't want," he continued, "is a starry-eyed girl who dreams of balls and gowns and handsome suitors. A marriage with such a frivolous creature would be a recipe for disaster."

Helena bristled. "That isn't fair, sir."

"Excuse me?"

"I'm no starry-eyed girl. I never was. And with respect, Mr. Boothroyd, you haven't the slightest notion of my dreams. If I wanted balls and gowns or...or frivolous things...I'd never have answered Mr. Thornhill's advertisement."

"What exactly do you seek out of this arrangement, Miss Reynolds?"

She clasped her hands tightly in her lap to stop their trembling. "Security," she answered honestly. "And perhaps...a little kindness."

"You couldn't find a gentleman who met these two requirements in London?"

"I don't wish to be in London. Indeed, I wish to be as far from London as possible."

"You friends and family...?"

"I'm alone in the world, sir."

"I see."

Helena doubted that very much. "Mr. Boothroyd, if you've already decided someone else is better suited—"

"There is no one else, Miss Reynolds. At present, you're the only lady Mr. Finchley has recommended."

"But the woman who was here before—"

"Mrs. Standish?" Mr. Boothroyd removed his spectacles. "She was applying for the position of housekeeper at the Abbey." He rubbed the bridge of his nose. "Regrettably, we have an ongoing issue with retaining adequate staff. It's something you should be aware of if you intend to take up residence."

She exhaled slowly. "A housekeeper. Of course. How silly of me. Mr. Thornhill mentioned the difficulties you were having with servants in one of his letters."

"I'm afraid it's proven quite a challenge." Mr. Boothroyd settled his spectacles back on his nose. "Not only is the house isolated, it has something of a local reputation. Perhaps you've heard...?"

"A little. But Mr. Finchley told me it was nothing more than ignorant superstition."

"Quite so. However, in this part of the world, Miss Reynolds, you'll find ignorance is in ready supply."

Helena was unconcerned. "I should like to see the Abbey for myself."

"Yes, yes. All in good time."

"And I should like to meet Mr. Thornhill."

"Undoubtedly." Mr. Boothroyd shuffled through his papers again. To her surprise, a rising color crept into the elderly man's face. "There are just one or two more points at issue, Miss Reynolds." He cleared his throat. "You're aware, I presume... That is, I do hope Mr. Finchley explained...this marriage is to be a real marriage in every sense of the word."

She looked at him, brows knit in confusion. "What other kind of marriage would it be?"

"And you're agreeable?"

"Of course."

He made no attempt to disguise his skepticism. "There are many ladies who would find such an arrangement singularly lacking in romance."

Helena didn't doubt it. She'd have balked at the prospect herself once. But much had changed in the past year—and in the past months, especially. Any girlish fantasies she'd harbored about true love were dead. In their place was a rather ruthless pragmatism.

"I don't seek romance, Mr. Boothroyd. Only kindness. And Mr. Finchley said that Mr. Thornhill was a kind man."

Mr. Boothroyd appeared to be surprised by this. "Did he indeed," he murmured. "What else did he tell you, pray?"

She hesitated before repeating the words that Mr. Finchley had spoken. Words that had convinced her once and for all to travel to a remote coastal town in Devon, to meet and marry a complete stranger. "He told me that Mr. Thornhill had been a soldier, and that he knew how to keep a woman safe."

Justin Thornhill cast another brooding glance at the pale, dark-haired beauty sitting across from Boothroyd. She was slight but shapely, her modest traveling gown doing nothing to disguise the high curve of her breasts and the narrow lines of her small waist. When first he'd seen her in the taproom, he thought she was a fashionable traveler on her way to Abbot's Holcombe, the resort town farther up the coast. He had no reason to think otherwise. The Miss Reynolds he'd been expecting—the plain, sensible spinster who'd responded to his matrimonial advertisement—had never arrived.

This Miss Reynolds was a different class of woman altogether.

She sat across from Boothroyd, her back ramrod straight, and her elegant, gloved hands folded neatly on her lap in a pretty attitude. She regarded the curmudgeonly steward with wide, doelike hazel eyes and when she spoke, she did so in the smooth, cultured tones of a gentlewoman. No, Justin amended. Not a gentlewoman. A *lady*.

She was nothing like the two sturdy widows Boothroyd had interviewed earlier for the position of housekeeper. Those women had, ironically, been more in line with Justin's original specifications—the specifications he had barked at his aging steward those many months ago when Boothroyd had first broached the idea of his advertising for a wife.

"I have no interest in courtship," he'd said, "nor in weeping young ladies who take to their bed with megrims. What I need is a woman. A woman who is bound by law and duty to see to the running of this godforsaken mausoleum. A woman I can bed on occasion. Damnation, Boothroyd, I didn't survive six years in India so I could live like a bloody monk when I returned home."

They were words spoken in frustration after the last in a

long line of housekeepers had quit without notice. Words that owed a great deal to physical loneliness and far too many glasses of strong spirits.

The literal-minded Boothroyd had taken them as his marching orders.

The next morning, before Justin had even arisen from his alcohol-induced slumber, his ever-efficient steward had arranged for an advertisement to be placed in the London papers. It had been brief and to the point:

MATRIMONY: Retired army officer, thirty-two, of moderate means and quiet disposition wishes to marry a spinster or widow of the same age. Suitable lady will be sensible, compassionate, and capable of managing the household of remote country property. Independent fortune unimportant. Letters to be addressed, postpaid, to Mr. T. Finchley, Esq., Fleet Street.

Justin had initially been angry. He'd even threatened to give Boothroyd the sack. However, within a few days he'd found himself warming to the idea of acquiring a wife by advertisement. It was modern and efficient. As straightforward as any other business transaction. The prospective candidates would simply write to Thomas Finchley, Justin's London attorney, and Finchley would negotiate the rest, just as competently as he'd negotiated the purchase of Greyfriar's Abbey or those shares Justin had recently acquired in the North Devon Railway.

Still, he had no intention of making the process easy. He'd informed both Boothroyd and Finchley that he would not bestir himself on any account. If a prospective bride wanted to meet, she would have to do so at a location within easy driving distance of the Abbey.

He'd thought such a condition would act as a deterrent.

It hadn't occurred to him that women routinely traveled such distances to take up employment. And what was his matrimonial advertisement if not an offer for a position in his household?

In due time, Finchley had managed to find a woman for whom an isolated existence in a remote region of coastal Devon sounded agreeable. Justin had even exchanged a few brief letters with her. Miss Reynolds hadn't written enough for him to form a definite picture of her personality, nor of her beauty—or lack thereof. Nevertheless, he'd come to imagine her as a levelheaded spinster. The sort of spinster who would endure his conjugal attentions with subdued dignity. A spinster who wouldn't burst into tears at the sight of his burns.

The very idea that anything like this lovely young creature would grace his table and his bed was frankly laughable.

Not but that she wasn't determined.

Though that was easily remedied. Folding his paper, Justin rose from his chair. "I'll take it from here, Boothroyd."

Miss Reynold's eyes lifted to his. He could see the exact moment when she realized who he was. To her credit, she didn't cry or faint or spring from her chair and bolt out of the room. She merely looked at him in that same odd way she had in the taproom when first she beheld his burns.

"Miss Reynolds," Mr. Boothroyd said, "may I present Mr. Thornhill?"

She did rise then and offered him her hand. It was small and slim, encased in a fine dark kid glove. "Mr. Thornhill."

"Miss Reynolds." His fingers briefly engulfed hers. "Sit down, if you please." He took Boothroyd's chair, waiting until his loyal retainer had removed himself to the other side of the parlor before fixing his gaze on his prospective bride.

Her face was a flawless, creamy porcelain oval, framed by dark brown hair swept back into an oversized roll at the nape of her neck. Her nose was straight—neither too short, nor too long—and her gently rounded chin was firm to the point of stubbornness. If not for the velvety softness of those doe eyes, she might have appeared prideful or even haughty. And perhaps she was, if her clothing was anything by which to judge.

Granted, he knew nothing of women's fashion—aside from the fact that the hooks, laces, and miles of skirts were dashed inconvenient when one was in an amorous frame of mind. But one didn't have to know the difference between a petticoat and a paletot to recognize that everything Miss Reynolds wore was of the finest quality. Even the tiny buttons on her bodice and the fashionable belt and buckle that encircled her waist appeared to have been crafted by a master.

Next to her, the suit of clothes he'd chosen to wear that morning to meet his intended bride felt rather shabby and third rate. Far worse, he was beginning to feel a little shabby and third rate himself.

"You'll forgive the deception," he said. "As you can see, I'm not the sort of man a woman would wish to find at the other end of a matrimonial advertisement."

"Aren't you?" She tilted her head. The small movement brought her hair in the path of a shaft of sunlight filtering in through the parlor window. It glittered for an instant in her fashionable coiffure, revealing threads of red and gold among the brown. "Why do you say so? Is it because of your burns?"

He was hard-pressed to conceal a flinch. Damn, but she was blunt. He wouldn't have expected such plain speaking from a decorative little female. "You can't claim the sight doesn't offend you. I saw your reaction in the taproom."

Her brows drew together in an elegant line. "I had no reaction, sir."

"No?"

"I was, perhaps, a little surprised. But not because of your burns." Her cheeks flushed a delicate shade of rose. "You are...very tall."

His chest tightened. He was uncertain what to make of her blushes—or of her personal remark. She was such a finely made little creature. He wondered if she thought him too big. Good God, he *was* too big. And too rough, too coarse, and too common and a host of other negative traits, the distastefulness of which he had not fully appreciated until being in her presence.

"You were expecting someone shorter?"

"No, I...I didn't know what to expect. How could I have? You never mentioned anything of that sort in your letters."

Justin recalled the polite and wholly impersonal letters he'd written to her over the past months. He'd described Greyfriar's Abbey, the seasons and the weather and the sound of the waves hitting the rocks beneath the cliffs. He'd mentioned the repairs to the roof, the new outbuildings, and the persistent trouble with keeping servants.

His own appearance hadn't merited a single line.

"Would you still have come, had you known?" he asked.

"About your burns, do you mean?" She didn't hesitate. "Yes, I think so. But there's no way to prove it now, is there? You shall have to take my word for it."

He allowed his gaze to drift over her face, taking in every feature, from the dark mahogany brows winging over her wide-set eyes, to the gentle curve of her cheekbones, and down to the impossibly sensual bow of her upper lip. It was not the face of a woman who had to answer a matrimonial advertisement in order to find a husband.

Take her word for it? "I suppose I must," he said.

"Did it happen while you were in India?"

He nodded once. "During the uprising."

"I didn't like to assume." She paused. "I know something of soldiers from my brother. He often wrote to me about the exploits of his regiment and the hardships of friends who'd been injured in battle. He was a soldier himself, you see."

"Was he, indeed?" Justin regarded her with a thoughtful expression. "I understood that you had no family."

"I don't. Not any longer. My brother was lost last year at the siege of Jhansi." Her bosom rose and fell on an unsteady breath. He noticed for the first time that she was trembling. "Is that where you were hurt, Mr. Thornhill?"

It wasn't a subject he enjoyed discussing, but there was no point in dissembling. She would find out soon enough. "No, at Cawnpore in '57."

Something flickered briefly in the velvet depths of her eyes. Everyone in England knew what had happened in Cawnpore during the uprising, but as the sister of a soldier, she'd have a better understanding than most.

"Were you serving under Major General Sir Hugh

Wheeler?" she asked very quietly. "Or did you arrive later, with Brigadier General Neill?"

"The former." His mouth curved into a mocking half smile. "You may rest easy, Miss Reynolds. I had no part in the raping and pillaging engaged in by the relieving forces. I was safely tucked away in an enemy prison at the time, being flayed alive by rebel sepoys." She blanched, but he didn't spare her. "The burns and scars you see here are nothing. The ones beneath my clothing are much, much worse, I assure you."

"I am very sorry for it."

"Are you?" He felt an unreasonable surge of anger toward her. "You may not feel quite so much Christian charity toward my scarred body when it's covering you in our marriage bed."

From his place across the room, Boothroyd emitted a strangled groan.

Justin ignored him. His attention was fixed on the scalding blush that swept from the slender column of Miss Reynold's porcelain throat all the way up to her hairline. Doubtless he'd shocked her virginal soul to its very core. He wouldn't have been surprised if she leapt up and slapped his face. He certainly deserved it.

But she did not strike him.

Instead, she met his insolent gaze and held it, unflinching.

"You're purposefully offensive, sir. I believe you're trying to scare me off. I cannot think why."

Because if you don't leave of your own accord, very soon I won't let you leave at all.

And where would he be then?

Stuck at Greyfriar's Abbey, among the crumbling stone

and cracked plaster, with a very unhappy lady. A lady reduced to drudgery in a drafty, damp, understaffed ruin. A lady whom he could never hope to satisfy, not if he lived to be one hundred.

"Perhaps," he said finally, "because it seems to me that you have no idea what you're getting yourself into."

"Nonsense. I know exactly what I'll get out of this arrangement. I wouldn't be here otherwise. If you don't wish to marry me, Mr. Thornhill, you need only say so."

"I wonder that you wish to marry me." He folded his arms and leaned back in his chair, surveying the neat little figure hidden beneath her gown. "I hope you're not in trouble, Miss Reynolds."

He heard her catch her breath. The sound was unmistakable.

His heart sank. There was no other way to describe it. The disappointment he felt was that exquisitely painful.

And then, just as swiftly, his temper flared.

"I may be acquiring a wife in a somewhat unconventional way, madam," he informed her in the same frigid accents he'd often employed with disrespectful subordinates in India, "but I have no desire to take on another man's bastard in the bargain."

Her mouth fell open. "*What?*"

"I believe you heard me." He moved to rise.

"You think I'm carrying *a child*?"

Something in her voice stopped him where he stood. He searched her face. "Do you deny it?"

"Yes!" She was blushing furiously now. "The suggestion is patently absurd. As well as being utterly impossible."

Absurd as well as impossible? His conscience twinged. So, she was an innocent after all. Either that or the finest actress he'd ever encountered in his life. "Ah," he said as he resumed his seat. "I see."

She raised a hand to brush a loose strand of hair from her face. She was trembling again.

"What kind of trouble is it, then?" he asked.

"I beg your pardon?"

"Something has plainly driven you to answer my advertisement. If not an unwanted child, then what?"

She dropped her gaze. Her long, thick lashes were black as soot against the creamy curve of her cheek. "You are mistaken, sir."

"And you are trembling, madam."

She immediately clasped her hands in her lap. "I always tremble when I'm nervous. I can't help it."

"Is that all that's wrong, Miss Reynolds? Nerves?"

Her lashes lifted and she met his eyes. "Does it really matter, Mr. Thornhill?"

He considered. "That depends. Have you broken the law?"

"Of course not. I simply wish to be married. It's why I answered your matrimonial advertisement. It's why I've come all this way. If you've decided I don't suit you—"

"You suit me." The words were out before he could call them back.

Try as he might, he could not regret them. It was the truth, by God. She was an uncommonly beautiful woman. He'd been physically attracted to her from the moment she came to stand beside him in the taproom.

On its own that wouldn't have been enough. He was no callow youth to have his head turned by a pretty face. But there was something else about her. Something lost and vulnerable and oddly courageous. It roused more than his ardor. It roused his protective instincts. It made him want to shield her from harm.

Is that why Finchley had sent her to him?

The very idea unsettled Justin deeply. He was no hero. Indeed, his own past conduct fairly disqualified him as a man capable of protecting a woman. Finchley *knew* that.

But if Justin had any lingering doubts about his decision, Miss Reynold's reaction to his pronouncement temporarily banished them from his mind.

Her face suffused with relief. Her soft hazel eyes glistened with what he very much feared were tears of gratitude. "You suit me as well," she said.

"Undoubtedly. Your requirements are not very exacting." He tugged at his collar. It felt damnably tight all of a sudden. "Security and a little kindness, is that right?"

"Yes, sir."

"And that I keep you safe."

"Yes, sir," she said. "That most of all."

About the Author

USA Today bestselling author Mimi Matthews writes both historical nonfiction and award-winning Victorian romances. Her novels have received starred reviews in *Publishers Weekly*, *Library Journal*, *Booklist*, *Kirkus*, and *Shelf Awareness*, and her articles have been featured on the *Victorian Web*, *the Journal of Victorian Culture*, and in syndication at *BUST Magazine*. In her other life, Mimi is an attorney. She resides in California with her family, which includes a retired Andalusian dressage horse, a Sheltie, and two Siamese cats.

Connect Online
MimiMatthews.com
Facebook: @MimiMatthewsAuthor
Instagram: @MimiMatthewsEsq
Twitter: @MimiMatthewsEsq

Want More?

Would you like to know when Mimi's next book is available? Sign up for her newsletter to keep up to date.

Join Mimi's exclusive Facebook group, Mimi Matthews' Victorian Reading Room, for exclusive access to Mimi as she shares her love of writing, historical romance, Victorian fashion, brooding heroes, independent heroines, and of course, her beloved pets!

Finally, the more reviews a book has, the more other readers will discover it. Every review helps, so if you have a moment to post your thoughts about this story, Mimi will be ever grateful.